THE WILD W

PIXIE
RING

TRAINING
GROUND

THE CABIN

THE ODDMIRE

SECRET
GOBLIN
PATH

THE
OĐĐMIRE

BOOK TWO

THE UNREADY QUEEN

THE
OĐĐMIRE

BOOK TWO
THE UNREADY QUEEN

written and illustrated by

William Ritter

Algonquin Young Readers   2020

Published by Algonquin Young Readers
an imprint of Algonquin Books of Chapel Hill
Post Office Box 2225
Chapel Hill, North Carolina 27515-2225

a division of Workman Publishing
225 Varick Street
New York, New York 10014

LIBRARY OF CONGRESS CATALOGING-IN-PUBLICATION DATA

Names: Ritter, William, 1984- author.
Title: The unready queen / written and illustrated by William Ritter.
Description: First edition. | Chapel Hill, North Carolina :
Algonquin Young Readers, 2020. | Series: The Oddmire ; book two |
Audience: Ages 8–12. | Audience: Grades 4–6. | Summary: Fable, the half-human
daughter of the Queen of the Deep Dark, and her friends, the human and goblin
brothers Cole and Tinn, discover that humans are destroying the Wild Wood,
breaking the unspoken truce between the people of Endsborough and the
inhabitants of the Wild Wood and leading them to war.
Identifiers: LCCN 2019057639 | ISBN 9781616208400 (hardcover) |
ISBN 9781643750644 (ebook)
Subjects: CYAC: Fairies—Fiction. | Forests and
forestry—Fiction. | Magic—Fiction. | Fantasy.
Classification: LCC PZ7.R516 Un 2020 | DDC [Fic]—dc23
LC record available at https://lccn.loc.gov/2019057639

10 9 8 7 6 5 4 3 2 1
First Edition

For Teresa.

You're magical, and I'm proud of you.

BEFORE

THERE ONCE WAS A WOMAN WHO LIVED DEEP IN the heart of the Wild Wood. She was fierce and fearless. And she was alone.

She did not miss people. People had turned their backs on her, and so she turned her back on them. When men from the nearby town set up camps or hunting blinds in her forest, the woman would turn more than just her back. She would turn big rocks and logs on them from the surrounding hills. It was her favorite hobby. Just before their tents were flattened, the men would hear the mad cackling of the woman in the woods.

Stories spread. The woman was a cursed thing. She was a witch. She had shared her soul with the forest to become the Queen of the Deep Dark. The woman heard these stories on the breeze and she breathed them in. She let them fill her up until she could burst. She became them.

But still, she remembered.

She remembered a child with bright hazel eyes and tiny, chubby fingers that reached out for hers. She remembered lullabies and good-night kisses—and she remembered a thief and an empty crib. The memories burned.

Every day the woman spoke her daughter's name on the breeze. *Raina.* Every day she gazed into the shadows of the forest, willing the darkness to surrender what had been taken from her. Every day, the forest gazed back.

Years passed. The woman learned to listen to the trees, and the trees learned to listen to her. If an animal was injured, the woman dressed its wounds. When hungry beasts of the Wild Wood came prowling, the woman stood tall and looked them in the eyes until they bowed their heads. The forest gradually bent to the will of the Queen of the Deep Dark.

But it could not give back what had been taken from her.

The woman grew old. Her hair became as white as daisy petals, and her hands shook. She knew the end was coming, but still she listened to the trees and cared for her creatures and defended her forest.

One quiet morning, the door to her cabin rattled on its hinges, and the woman rose with a start.

"If you've come to finish me off, get on with it," she snapped, stumping stiffly across the floor. "I haven't got all day. Or at least I wouldn't have all day if you'd stop dawdling."

She threw open the door.

There was nothing there but a dusty walkway of polished river rocks and the whisper of a breeze.

The woman sniffed the air.

"Better not be any thieving little goblins out here!" she yelled hoarsely. "I may be one foot in the grave, but don't think I won't drag a few of you with me. Hello?"

The wind died away and the forest crackled with invisible energy. The hairs on the woman's arms prickled. She held her breath. In front of her, the empty air opened with a clap of thunder, and a bulky shape tumbled out of nothing onto the forest floor.

Suddenly the woman was not alone.

There once was a child whom the goblins stole away. She was a sweet child with joyful dimples and thick curls of

3

rich brown hair. One night, her mother kissed her forehead tenderly and tucked her into her crib, and the next day the girl awoke in a palace full of glittering lights and heady aromas. She did not remember being secreted away through the forest by goblins. She did not remember being sold at a reasonable price to the fair folk. She did not remember crossing through an invisible gate to the wrong side of the veil (even after many years, it would always feel wrong), but she remembered that kiss, her mother's good-night kiss, long after she had grown. Some days, she could almost feel her mother's lips on her forehead, could almost hear her mother calling her name. *Raina.*

The fairies were not unkind. She was treated like a precious pet, fed meals that tasted like sweetened sunbeams, and clad in dresses that shimmered like starlight on water. The fairies loved her, in their way, and they called her Florabelle. It was a fine name, but it was not hers. Raina knew that it was not her name, although there were days she could barely remember what her real name was. There were days she nearly forgot herself completely.

Time passed more slowly in this place than it did on the earthly side of the veil, but still it passed.

As the child grew, the magic of the palace pressed up against her and she pressed up against it, until they began to grow as one. The fairies taught her spells and charms,

4

intrigued that a mortal was able to perform them. They looked on with pride, noticing that their human child had become something more than human. One particular fairy smiled all the more kindly as he noted that she had become something more than a child, as well. He was young by fairy standards and fair by any standard. He made no advances, but the girl called Florabelle found herself wishing that he would.

With time, childhood fell away from her completely, like a snakeskin, and what emerged was a woman of remarkable talents. Her handsome fairy waited. He did not age. He did not sour. When she was ready, she made her own advances. She slipped her hand into his and pressed her head against his chest. He did not protest.

There was a courtship and there was a wedding, and in time the woman called Florabelle conceived a child of her own. Her husband saw joy in her face, but also sadness. She confessed she did not want her baby to be born so far from her home. It pained him to hear her say it, but he promised her that he would take them back across the veil when the time came. He drew a map. He told her about a secret gate. Their child would know the Earth.

Florabelle's time approached, but the war approached faster. With their baby expected within the month, her husband was summoned away to defend the barrier. Florabelle begged him not to leave her, but he told her that he must. The fairy court had allowed his union to a human, but he was still fae. Rich or poor, male or female, it was the duty of all fair folk to defend the realm. Before he left, he gave her a gift. "If I should fall in battle," he told her, "take this and go—bring nothing else from this land with you."

Florabelle unfolded a thick, warm cloak of bearskin. It was rough and ragged, so unlike the silken gowns that filled her closet.

"Put it on before you leave this place," he told her, "for the way is cold and unforgiving."

And he left. The world shook. Days passed. Weeks. It became clear her husband was not coming back. Florabelle, whose true name had all but forgotten her, now shed her beautiful clothes and all her lovely trinkets. She kept nothing she had been given there, except that bearskin cloak, which she wrapped snugly around her shoulders.

And then the girl whom the goblins had stolen away finally stole herself back.

The frozen air bit her cheeks, but the cloak was warm against her skin as she slipped into the forest. In her belly, her baby kicked impatiently.

Miles passed under her bare feet. The sun dipped low in the sky, but she was nearing the passage—she could feel it. She was so close.

Noises erupted in the brush. Creatures lurked ahead. The musk of something vile crept through her nostrils: the stink of rot and the coppery scent of blood. Her heart pounded in her chest. A chill flooded through her like ice spreading across the surface of a stream. She could see flashes of teeth and talons between the branches, and for a moment she froze. She pulled the cloak tighter and slipped the hood over her head. As she did, she changed. She felt the hide settle heavily against her skin . . . and then settle a little deeper. She felt hot and powerful. The veil-gate was there, just ahead. It was ten feet away, atop a mossy mound in the forest. She took a deep breath and bounded toward it, paws hammering against the forest floor.

It was quiet on the human side of the veil, except for the gentle hum of insects and the whisper of a soft breeze through the leaves. In a world called Earth, in the middle of a thick forest known by the locals as the Wild Wood, a great brown bear erupted from the empty air and landed heavily on the leafy ground.

The bear breathed in deeply. She savored the smell of the wind and the dirt and the pine trees. Her head was spinning, and her eyes swam with tears. She was in a strange new wood in a strange new body, but for the first time in as long as she could remember, the world felt right. It felt like a warm embrace, like a tender kiss on her forehead. The forest rustled with excitement. It had been waiting, too.

The bear lifted her eyes to the golden sunlight and remembered. *Raina.* It was the name her mother had given her. *Raina.* It was a name that meant *queen*, and it was her name, and no one could take it from her.

Twigs snapped, and Raina turned around. A woman was standing in the clearing behind her, as thin as a birch tree, with soft white hair that caught the sunlight and fluttered in the breeze like cobwebs. The woman shook, but she did not shy away.

Slowly, the bear drew back her head, and her thick hide became a cloak once more. Rich brown curls fell across her shoulders as she lowered the hood.

For a long time, the two women gazed into each other's hazel eyes.

"Raina." The old woman's voice was barely a whisper. "You came home."

By week's end, the woman in the woods had died. Raina knelt and kissed her mother's forehead, and then she wept. The forest wept with her, and as they wept, the skies darkened and sheets of rain poured down the hills and flooded the valleys. The mire swelled and swallowed up the mossy glens around it, and creatures huddled in their burrows and dens as thunder shook the hills.

When at last there were no more tears to shed, the sun cut through the clouds and the Wild Wood wrapped itself around its long-lost daughter. Raina felt it settle on her shoulders like a mantle. Her mother's mantle. Her mantle, now. The Queen of the Deep Dark.

And then the contractions began.

ONE

AFTER THIRTEEN YEARS OF FALLING LEAVES AND creeping ivy, the clearing still had not changed. Not really. The moss was a little thicker, the trees a little taller.

An anxious wind swept through the high branches of the forest. Pine needles and birch leaves spun to the earth, and the bushes quivered with eager energy. The birds had stopped chirping, and even the insects had ceased their incessant buzzing. An uneasy quiet fell. The forest held its breath.

"Okay," said Raina, the Queen of the Deep Dark. "Your turn."

Fable swallowed. "It isn't going to work. They don't listen to me."

"They will."

"They never do."

"Try."

Fable took a deep breath. She scrunched up her eyes and focused on the sound of the leaves. The wind was dying down, and silence was settling over the woods like a blanket.

"Concentrate."

"I am."

"Listen."

"I *am* listening."

"You're not listening. You're trying too hard."

"You told me to try!"

"Just listen."

"I'm listening. *They* don't listen to *me*!"

"Just breathe."

"I'm breathing."

"And concentrate."

"MOTHER, I AM LISTENING AND BREATHING AND CONCENTRATING!"

The entire forest shuddered, and birds erupted into the sky all around them. Like a dam breaking, the myriad sounds of the Wild Wood rushed back over the clearing. A single bright green leaf spun lazily down to land atop Fable's frizzy curls. She snatched it off her head and tore it up.

"This is stupid." Fable kicked a pinecone across the forest. "Why do we even have to practice listening to stupid trees?"

"Listening is the most important skill a queen must master. When you listen to the trees, they will listen to you."

"The trees don't ever listen to me. The forest doesn't even like me."

"It will. You just haven't gotten your roots in yet. You will grow, like the Grandmother Trees near the forest's four corners. They are pillars of the forest, Fable, just as you will someday be a pillar. They are sturdy, and their roots are deep. They know where they stand, and so no wind can blow them over. You need to feel the roots beneath you and come to know where you stand."

"I know where I'm standing. I'm standing in the middle of your vine circle for the millionth time practicing the same spells as always, even though they never work."

"Magic takes time."

"Not *my* magic! *My* magic is easy!"

"Fable, please."

"I can transform! I can do slappy sparks!"

"No." The queen was firm. "You are not practicing spark again until you've gotten better at extinguish."

"Ugh." Fable rolled her eyes. "I've spent hours on extinguish. I can't do it."

"You just have to learn to reach—"

"—*reach out for the flame in my mind and grasp it with a hand that cannot be burned*," Fable recited in her mother's voice. "I know. You've said it a million times. Pretty sure I don't have the same fireproof brain-hand that you have."

"You do. The magic is in your veins. But real magic requires discipline."

"What do you mean *real* magic? I can do *real* magic! Last week I turned a pinecone into a hedgehog!"

"And you were only trying to make it spin! That's my point! Fable, it's not enough to have power if you don't know how to use it, how to do it on purpose—how to *un*do it if necessary."

"You want me to turn Squidge *back* into a pinecone?" Fable gasped. "But she *loves* being a hedgehog!"

"I don't want you to do anything to Squidge." The queen pinched the bridge of her nose and sighed. "I want you to concentrate on your lessons. What about compel? You've made real progress with compel."

Fable took a deep breath. "You want me to try to make stuff move with my brain again?"

"I prefer to think of it as *strongly encouraging* things to move, but yes. Let's review first. What sorts of things can you compel?"

"Pretty much nothing," said Fable. "Because it's hard and it never works right."

"What *could* you move," the queen pressed, "if it *did* work?"

Fable fiddled with a patch of sap in her hair as she echoed the lessons she had been taught for years. "Stones and other minerals are difficult to compel because their energy is stubborn. Wind and water can be compelled more easily by redirecting their natural currents. Plants can also be compelled, because their growth and subtle movements need only be"—she gave her mother a sidelong glance—"*strongly encouraged* to move more quickly or to take on specific shapes."

"Good," said the queen. "And . . . ?"

"And living creatures are nearly impossible to compel, although some insects will succumb to suggestion, like ants."

"That's right. Not all insects, though. Ladybugs are surprisingly strong-willed."

"Birds and reptiles and other more complex animals might feel the push, but generally ignore it unless otherwise motivated," Fable rattled on. "And people cannot be compelled at all."

"Correct." The queen gave a nod. "Why not?"

"Something about how a person's life force is like a rushing current, too strong to be turned from its course."

"Excellent."

"Have you ever tried?"

"Tried?" the queen said.

"*Compelling* a person. Have you ever tried?"

"Manipulating a human being against their will would be wrong," said the queen.

"That means you did! If you hadn't you would just say *no*." Fable grinned. "How'd it go?"

The queen pursed her lips. "I would have a much easier time keeping interlopers out of our forest if it had gone well," she admitted. "You cannot compel a human being. It would require unimaginable power to elicit even the tiniest reaction."

"What about dead people?"

"Fable!"

"What? I'm not gonna *do* it."

"We do not meddle with that manner of magic. Not ever. When you cast a spell over something, you enter into an exchange. For a short time, you share your energy—you welcome in the essence of the subject you are compelling. When you compel a tree, you *become* the tree, and the tree becomes you."

15

"So compelling dead stuff would make me part dead?"

The queen's expression was dark. "More or less," she answered. "Let's try something lighter, shall we? What do we call it when we compel the wind?"

"Gale," said Fable without enthusiasm. "But you know gale is one of my worst spells. I'm not going to be able to do it."

"You will. Just take a deep breath through your lungs and let it out on the breeze."

Fable took a deep breath in, and blew it out again.

"Try again."

Another deep breath.

"That's it. Now let it out on the breeze."

Fable's face began to turn red. "Ugh!" she finally burst. "There's only two ways air comes out of me, Mama. The front way and the back way—and you never think the back way is as funny as I do."

"You'll get it. You just have to develop a bond with the forest first. You need to connect with it."

A pinecone sailed down from the canopy above them and caught Fable hard on the head.

"Ow!" She glowered at the trees. They swayed innocently above her. "See?" she demanded. "This is dumb! Nature is dumb! Just open the wild-wall so I can go."

The queen sighed. "One more time."

"No! I don't want to *listen* or *breathe* or *concentrate*. I don't want to become a pillar like the stupid Grandmother Trees. And I don't want to talk to your jerk forest. You said I could visit Tinn and Cole today."

The queen frowned. "Yes. I did. I think perhaps that was a mistake. You have been spending a lot of time—"

"No take-backs!"

Fable stomped up to the wall of foliage her mother had grown all around them for privacy. It was easy for her mother. The plants listened to the queen. The animals listened to the queen. Everybody listened to the queen. Nobody listened to Fable. With each practice session she had suffered, her mother's wall of greenery had felt less and less like a protection and more and more like a prison.

"One more time first," the queen pressed.

"Why? One more time to feel stupid? One more time to get it wrong?"

"Yes. We learn more from how we get it wrong—"

"—*than we learn from getting it right*," Fable droned. "You *always* say that, but I still haven't learned *anything*. Just open the bushes, Mama."

"Why don't you open them?" the queen prompted. "Just try. Compel the vines. You're strong enough. I know you are."

Fable clenched her fists. "You're right," she said. "I am strong enough." And with that, she spun on her heel, and where a girl had stood moments before now perched a bear cub, balancing on its hind legs.

The queen pursed her lips. "Fable, no."

The cub narrowed her eyes. The queen sighed. Fable would not be her little cub much longer. Already the child was growing into her flank, her paws looking less adorably overlarge and more suited to her size every day.

In a flurry of motion, the cub shredded the branches in front of her until they were nothing but ragged splinters, and then she stormed off through the gap.

"Violence is not the same thing as strength!" the queen called after her. Fable did not respond. The queen sagged. "She will learn," she told herself.

The leaves rustled skeptically above her.

Footsteps crunched toward the tattered gap in the foliage. The queen looked up. "Fable?"

The face that peered around the corner was neither human nor cub.

"I take it today didn'a go any better'n yesterday, eh, witchy?" The drab green goblin removed his battered top hat as he stepped into the clearing. Nudd, High Chief of the Hollowcliff Horde, was half the queen's height, but he bore himself with all the confidence of his regal station. He had come alone. He always came alone.

"My family's concerns are none of yours, Thief King," the queen answered coldly.

"Ya know as well as I do that that child is a concern of every last creature in the Wild Wood."

The queen did not reply.

"Otch. I didn'a come ta hassle ya, Raina. We're on the same side. Tell me—is she learning ta control it at all?"

The queen hesitated before she spoke. "She will. She just has too much of her mother in her."

Nudd smirked. "Aye, that's the truth. An' a good thing, too. She'll need plenty o' that if she's ta last long in this forest. But 'tis the *something else* she's got inside o' her that has me twitchy."

The queen took a deep breath. She should never have told Nudd. It was her story—hers and Fable's and no one else's—but there was no un-telling a story once it had been told.

"They taught me how to control it," she said. "I will teach my daughter."

"Ah, but you were just a wee human lass with a bit o' magic under yer skin. Yer daughter is something else— she's a part o' *them*, through an' through."

"My daughter is human."

"Human *plus* . . ." Nudd said. "That's dangerous magic, theirs. Stronger'n the Wild Wood is used to. 'Twas yer own mother who taught these trees ta trust neither humans nor fair folk—an' yer wee Fable is both. Dangerous combination, that. The forest hasn'a decided what ta do with her yet."

The queen's brow furrowed. "Fable is not a danger to the Wild Wood."

"Na?" Nudd countered. "There's plenty would say that *you're* the most dangerous thing in these woods, an' she's already more powerful than you are. Least you can control yourself."

"She is not more powerful than I am." But even as the queen said it, she pulled the bearskin cloak tighter around herself. She could take animal form, but only through the magic of the cloak. Fable had been able to transform at will since she was barely able to walk. Spark had been one of the most difficult spells Raina had learned to cast in her childhood. Snuffing a flame had been relatively easy— but creating one out of nothing had taken years to master. Little Fable had worked out how to do it when she was five. By seven she had nearly set the Wild Wood on fire a dozen times. Wild, unruly magic had always been effortless to Fable, yet structured magic—courtly magic—the queen's magic—remained a brick wall to her. "She will learn."

"When?" Nudd's eyebrows rose. The pale scar that ran through one brow and down his cheek wrinkled. "Yer wee witchling was, what, twelve last summer when she tussled with the fabric o' the universe itself? And *won*?"

The queen swallowed.

"She still makin' flowers turn inta butterflies by accident?"

The queen said nothing.

"Mm-hm. What clever trick will she stumble into when she's sixteen? Twenty? I'm na blind, witchy. I can see she's gettin' stronger. So can the rest o' the forest folk. What will happen when she's na some wee thing any-more? What will happen when her mother's na around ta look after her—when the forest becomes hers ta protect? Or do ya think she'll handle that moment smoothly when it comes?"

The queen said nothing.

Nudd relented, and the two of them listened wordlessly to the birds bickering and squawking at one another for a few minutes.

"She is a good lass, Raina," the chief said at last, more gently. "She does have a lot of her mother in her."

The queen nodded.

"We're having the boy over," the chief added, more lightly. "The changeling, Tinn. Poor lad doesn'a know the

21

first thing about his own kind. Got ta learn about his heritage somehow."

The queen arched an eyebrow. "Does he, though?" Tinn had been raised by humans his entire life—he looked human, acted human, thought of himself as human—but he was not human. A goblin named Kull had tried to steal a baby from town by swapping it for a goblin changeling, but he had botched the whole affair, leaving both human and changeling behind. The boys had grown up as twins, made indistinguishable by the ancient magic. Not even the boys had known for sure which of them was the doppelgänger until last summer.

"Course he does." Nudd nodded. "He'll be spendin' his first night with the horde this week's end. Kull is just about sick, he's so excited for it."

"Very brave of Annie to relinquish her son for the night."

"Oh, aye. She's put the horde on pain of death iffin he comes back in fewer pieces than she lent him." Nudd chuckled. "Ya know," he added in the careful tone of one who wishes to appear as though an idea he has been carrying for days has only just occurred to him, "we could take the girl, too."

The queen raised an eyebrow.

"Maybe yer witchy way just isn'a what the lass needs right now. She's na what you were, Raina. We goblins may na be fair folk, but we do know our own way around magic. Be right honored ta tutor the future Queen o' the Deep Dark."

The queen regarded Nudd for several seconds. "Thank you, Thief King. But I trust that you will understand when I say no child of mine will ever be taken by goblins without bloodshed."

Nudd's lips cracked open in a full, broad grin—his jagged teeth parting as he cackled. "Ha! Yer mother would be right proud ta hear ya say it. Sound just like her. You've got more'n a little of her in you, too, ya know. I see it most when yer threatenin' my life. It's in the eyes, I think. Fine woman, she was. Fine woman. She could cuss like poetry."

The queen allowed herself a smile.

"Well, the offer stands, iffin ya change yer mind." Nudd pulled the top hat back down over his floppy ears. "Ya know where ta find me, Raina."

"Never forget that I do, Thief King."

Nudd gave the woman a wink and clambered back out over the ruined shrubbery. The queen watched him go before sitting down against a coil of mossy roots. The chief was not wrong. Ever since the night of the Veil Moon— the night Fable had reached inside the gap between realities—the girl's powers had gotten more unpredictable. She was still the same Fable, for better or worse, but lately the universe had begun responding.

Last week, Fable had slept poorly and had yelled at a chirruping jay in the early hours of the morning. The birdsong had ended abruptly—not because the bird had stopped singing, but because it had stopped being a bird. An exceptionally confused iguana had fallen out of the tree where the jay had been. It had taken the queen all morning to unravel the spell, and the bird that had flown away in the end still looked rather greener than it should have.

More troubling still had been when the queen asked Fable to help pull the withered black brambles from between the Oddmire and the gully. It was a task that should have taken all day, wrenching the dead things from the earth and burning them all in careful piles. By midmorning they were gone. Just gone. The vines had been unmade. Not that the queen had any interest in restoring the wretched plants, but it unnerved her that she could not have done so even if she tried. There was no spell to unravel. They had simply been dismissed from reality, and Fable didn't seem to realize what she had done.

The queen closed her eyes and took a deep breath. Fable *was* a good girl. She just had to learn control.

Beneath the queen, the earth trembled.

TWO

"YOU DON'T HAVE TO WALK US ALL THE WAY TO school," Tinn said as they made their way down the dusty Endsborough sidewalk.

"We're thirteen now," agreed Cole. "Lots of kids our age have jobs already."

"I'm well aware that you two are thirteen," Annie answered. "I baked the cake." She sighed. Already the boys could wear their mother's work boots when they needed to tromp around the garden, and it would not be very many birthdays before they were taller than she was. They still looked astonishingly similar—aside from Annie, nobody in town could tell the twins apart on sight—but she could not help but notice that they were growing more different every day.

From the very first day she had found them together in their crib, Annie's boys had been identical to the last freckle. It used to be that if one boy scuffed his chin, the other came back an hour later with a mark to match. That had been the mysterious power of the changeling at work, but Annie had grown accustomed to her boys being mirror images of each other. Lately, though, Cole had taken to wearing his hair pushed back, and had even used his birthday money to try out some of the pomade hair treatment that Mr. Zervos sold in the general store. The fashion made him look older—and rather like his father, though he didn't know it, which pulled on Annie's heart. Tinn, on the other hand, kept his hair loose and shaggy, and so low it brushed his eyebrows. It still made him smile when Annie ruffled it. Cole's shoulders seemed just a little broader than his brother's, and he stood just a hair taller—but that might have been due to Tinn's tendency to slouch. Tinn had always been the more timid of the two. Learning the truth—that he was human merely by virtue of magic—had only amplified his anxious nature. They were still her boys, through and through, and neither age nor magic could ever change that.

"We could, you know," said Cole.

"Hm?" Annie replied. "Could what?"

"Get jobs," Cole said. "I know you don't have a lot saved up."

"You worry about your schooling," Annie answered. "Let me worry about money." They walked on a few more paces. "What makes you think I haven't got enough saved up, anyhow?"

The boys exchanged glances.

"It's just," said Tinn, hesitantly, "not everything is good when it's canned."

"Raspberry jam is great," added Cole, hastily.

"Everybody loves jam."

"But then there's the green beans. And the carrots."

"The carrots were when I knew," agreed Tinn.

Annie rolled her eyes. "There's nothing wrong with canned vegetables."

"Yeah, but even you hate mushy carrots," said Cole.

Annie sighed. "Only because they are the worst food ever created. All right. Yes, we have been running a bit light. But I've already begun looking for part-time work. There are always a few odd jobs to be done in town. Just let me worry about that. We'll be fine."

"I thought you already had a job," said Tinn, "making pies for Mr. Barmbrack."

Annie nodded. "It turns out, a bit of baking twice a

week does not make enough to keep up with two hungry young men."

"And the thing with the chairs?" asked Cole.

"Caning chairs helped us make it through last winter, but there are only so many seats in Endsborough. I'm just going to have to try to find something that's a bit more regular."

Tinn winced involuntarily at the word. If there was anything his family was not good at, it was *regular*.

They came up to the broad building in the center of town that was Endsborough's schoolhouse, church, and grange hall, as occasion demanded. A handful of children were milling about near the entrance. Cole waved to Hana and Oscar. *Their* mothers had not walked *them* all the way to school.

Off to the left of the front doors was a weathered public message board. Annie stepped up to it and regarded the postings. "Let's see. Farmhand. Cattle driver. Goodness, not for me, I think. Oh, here's one. Mr. Zervos has a listing for a clerk at the general store. I could be the sort of person who works in a shop, don't you think?"

Cole had stopped paying attention. His scanning eyes had landed on a faded ad for positions with the Echo Point Mining Company. His father had worked in the mines—right up until the day he disappeared. Cole and Tinn had only been babies, but people still talked about it from time to time, mostly when they thought the twins could not hear them. The story was that Joseph Burton clocked out at Echo Point, picked up his lunch box, and never arrived home. Cole bristled. Their mother would not be stretching herself thin for every opportunity to mend busted chairs or sell baked beans if her husband had not abandoned her.

"Pardon me, ladies and gentlemen, pardon me."

Cole pulled his attention away from the flyer as a middle-aged man in a tweed suit and a straw boater strode up to the message board with a sheet of paper in his hands.

"There's a good lad. Thank you, son, just squeezing in. Won't be a moment." The man patted Cole on the shoulder genially as the boys stepped out of the way. "Couple of strapping young men you've got with you today, ma'am," he called over his shoulder to Annie.

"Thank you, sir. They're good boys. Sometimes."

The man chuckled and went to work banging a tack into each corner of the paper. His flyer was crisp and brighter than the other postings, printed on smooth paper in three different fancy styles of lettering. "That should do it." The man took a step back and gave his work a satisfied nod.

Cole and Tinn peered around his elbows on either side to read what the flyer said. It was for a job at a construction project out past the old mill.

"What's a *pump jack*?" said Tinn.

"*What's a pump jack?*" echoed the man. "Why, my boy, it's the future of your sleepy town! It is technological progress in a bold new age."

"It's a great big machine for drawing oil," Annie clarified.

"Right you are, ma'am! Spot on!" The man gave Annie a broad smile. "*Black gold*, we call it. We're building a machine to pull profits right out of the dirt. Good as a golden goose. Hold on, now. Where are my manners? I don't believe we've met."

"Annie Burton," said Annie Burton. "And I take it you're Mr. Hill?" She nodded to the flyer, which had JACOB HILL written in bold block letters across the top.

"Right again, my dear. Most astute." Mr. Hill held out a hand and Annie shook it politely. "Looking for some after-school work, boys?" Hill asked, turning to the twins.

Cole was ready to answer when Annie replied for both of them. "I think they're a bit young to be working with heavy machinery."

"We're not too young," Cole grumbled. "I would look out for Tinn and Tinn would look out for me."

"Mother knows best, boys," Hill said with a shrug. "Never too early to pick up a trade, though. At their age I was already working for my uncle. You lads ever heard of Dr. Emerson's Enervating Elixirs?"

The twins shook their heads.

"Might be for the best." Hill leaned in conspiratorially. "Just between you and me, his treatments smelled like feet and tasted like garlic and peaches." He chuckled. "But I learned more on the road selling stinky tonics than ever I did in a classroom."

"Mm. Worldly advice, thank you," said Annie.

"Well, if you change your mind, I'm operating out of the town inn for the time being," said Hill. "Always room for a few steady hands. You boys mind your mother, now. Pleasure meeting you all." He gave them a nod and turned to go.

"Hi, Mr. Hill," called a girl's voice coming from the other direction.

Tinn stiffened. Evie Warner and her father were making their way toward the schoolhouse. His mouth went dry. Tinn's words always got tangled up when he tried to talk to Evie Warner. She never seemed to mind, which only made it worse, somehow. He felt suddenly that he should be doing *something* with his hands, but could not for the life of him think what.

"Good morning, young lady," Hill answered, with a tip of his boater. "Ah, Oliver. I'm glad I ran into you."

Evie's father greeted Hill with a handshake.

Evie waved to Annie and the boys. "Hi, Mrs. Burton," she said. "Hi, guys."

"Hey, Evie," said Cole.

"Hello, hi, howdy, hi," said Tinn, and then immediately wished he hadn't said anything. His tongue felt enormous.

"Lots to do today, Oliver," Hill was saying behind them. "Lots to do! All hands on deck. We'll be rolling up our sleeves to get that field clear. Might even recruit your little Evie by the end of the week."

Evie giggled. "Pretty sure I wouldn't be much help clearing a field." She looked down at herself as if presenting evidence. Evie was small—smaller than all the other kids in her class and most of the ones several grades younger. She had been to a doctor in New Fiddleham who said she wasn't ever going to get much taller.

"Hey, now." Hill gave her a wink. "I've never been the biggest or the strongest either, kid. But I've always been a *people* person. That's what my old man taught me. *People are stronger together,* he used to say. *So make friends. Turn their strengths into your strength.* That's the secret. It means I get to recruit fine folks like your daddy and we both come out better for it in the end. Isn't that right, Oliver?"

"That's right, Mr. Hill." Oliver nodded.

"Speaking of making friends," Annie said, "all of you should be getting inside with the other kids now."

"Ah, right," said Oliver Warner. "Have a good day at school, Evie. Remember that Uncle Jim is going to be picking you up today. Your mama won't be back from her sister's for a few weeks yet, and I'll be working late with Mr. Hill."

"I remember. Love you, Daddy."

Children were filing into the schoolhouse, and Mrs. Silva had stepped outside to greet the class and shepherd the stragglers indoors.

"Off you go, boys," said Annie. "Have a good day, Evie."

"Thanks, Mrs. Burton," said Evie. "You, too!"

The bell clanged as the kids slipped inside the classroom.

"Your uncle's Jim Warner?" Cole said, sidling up to Evie.

"My great uncle." Evie nodded. "Yup."

"Wait, as in *Old Jim*?" said Tinn.

"The one with the apple orchard out by the edge of town?" added Cole.

"Yeah, that's him."

"I didn't know Old Jim was your uncle!" said Cole. "How weird is that!"

Evie shrugged. "He's pretty fun."

"Fun?" said Tinn. "Old Jim is *fun*?"

"Sure. He's got all kindsa stories about the Wild Wood. There's tons of creepy stuff out there. You guys have no idea."

Tinn and Cole shared a knowing glance.

"My parents usually make him stop right when he's getting to the best parts about body parts, or gushing blood, or monsters melting people with their spit," Evie continued, "but Mom's been away for a few weeks and Dad's been busy, so I've been spending more time at Uncle Jim's lately, and he's been telling all his stories extra gross, just for me. It's been fantastic."

"Whoa," said Tinn.

"Nice," said Cole.

"If you want, I'll tell you some of the best ones during recess."

Tinn grinned broadly as they walked up the aisle to their seats.

For the first time in a long time, Tinn felt happy. Ever since he was a baby, the story had hung over his head. Goblins tried to steal the Burton boy and replace him with a changeling, people said, but the goblins failed. The human and the monster got left together, except nobody could tell which was which—so poor Annie Burton had raised them both as brothers. One of the boys was a wicked thing. One of them was a parasite. One of them did not belong. Tinn had spent his whole life secretly worrying that he was *the one*. And then the answer had come.

It had been more than a month since their adventure in the Wild Wood, since Tinn had almost drowned in the murky Oddmire and nearly died in the Deep Dark. It had been more than a month since he had learned the terrible truth: that he was a goblin changeling and not a real boy at all. His whole world had been pulled out from under him—except his family had been there to catch him as he fell. His brother and mother had come back for him. They had stayed for him. Fought for him. And just like that, the nightmare had been over.

Now he was following Evie Warner up a row of beautifully boring wooden desks like none of it had ever happened. Tinn had come so close to losing everything and everybody he had known his whole life—he couldn't help but feel a bit giddy now that everything was back to normal. Better than normal.

A year ago, he could barely speak to Evie, but now— okay, he still had trouble stringing together more than a few words without stumbling all over them. But *she* was saying more to *him* lately, and Tinn could not have been happier about that.

He slid into the desk between Evie and Cole, right at the front of the room. He and his brother usually sat toward the back, out of sight, as unnoticed as possible until the bell rang and they hurried outside. Last week, however, Evie had invited them to sit near her. She always sat at the very front because she had trouble seeing the blackboard over the other students. Evie didn't hide herself away at the back of the room. This year, Tinn had decided to stop hiding, too.

Tinn had spent his whole life worrying that he was a freak. Somehow, finding out that it was true had made him more comfortable in his own skin than he had been when he didn't know. He could do this. He could be a regular kid.

The inkwell at the head of his desk had been slightly overfilled, and it sloshed as Tinn clambered into his seat. A drop of rich black india ink dripped down the side of the well.

"Whoops." Tinn wiped at the ink absently with his fingers before it could spread.

"Good morning, ladies and gentlemen," Mrs. Silva called, walking up the center aisle.

"Good morning, Mrs. Silva," the class replied as one.

"Take your seat, please, Hana. Thank you. Hat off, Oscar. Quiet, everyone. Quiet down. Okay. We will be starting with vocabulary all this week, so please have your workbooks out."

As the class shuffled into their places, Tinn glanced down at his fingers. The ink had made a jet-black stain about the size of a half-dollar. He blew on it to dry it.

"Page seven, please, everyone," announced Mrs. Silva. "Are we all there? Good. Eunice, would you read the instructions at the top of the page, please?"

Tinn flipped to page seven—but then froze, staring at his hand again. The mark on his fingers had spread halfway down his palm. Ugh. How? It had been only the smallest drop of ink. As he stared, the blackness crept farther, and with it grew a cold lump in Tinn's chest. That wasn't ink— his skin was changing.

No, no, no, he thought. *Not here. Not now.*

"Very good. Thank you, Eunice," Mrs. Silva said. "The first word is *abate*. Oscar, will you please read the definition of *abate* out loud for the class?"

Please stop. Please stop. Please stop, Tinn urged the stain, but the darkness continued expanding, wrapping around Tinn's fingers like an inky glove. He could feel the magic prickling across the back of his hand. *This can't be happening.* He stuffed his arm under his desk. His heart was pounding. Evie glanced over at him and Tinn felt sick. Had she seen? Had anybody seen? Why had he sat at the front of the class? This was a terrible idea. He needed to get out.

"Thank you, Oscar. Very good. The next word is *aberration*. Let's see. Tinn?"

"Huh? What?" Tinn's face felt clammy. Was it changing? Was his skin transforming right in front of his teacher, turning into shadowy obsidian like it had on that horrible night in the forest? It was, wasn't it? She was staring right at him.

"*Aberration*, Mr. Burton. If you don't mind." Mrs. Silva tapped his workbook. "Page seven."

"I—" The classroom was too hot and the walls were starting to spin. "I—" Everyone was definitely staring now. "I need to—bathroom. Please. I need to go to the bathroom. Now." He stumbled out of his desk, stuffing the treacherous hand under his armpit as he raced out of the room.

THREE

TINN TOOK DEEP BREATHS AS HE SLID INTO THE gap between the old supply shed and the back wall of the schoolhouse. He slumped down with his back against the cold bricks. The air was cool and earthy, and tall tufts of grass and wild daisies had grown up enough on either side to provide a natural blind in case any passersby should glance in his direction. He could still hear the quiet murmur of class in session on the other side of the wall, but it sounded far away, like it was somebody else's world and not his. Tinn put his head on his knees and tried not to cry.

Why was this happening *now*? For weeks after he had learned he was a changeling, Tinn had *tried* to do magic.

He had fantasized about what it might be like to control it. He had stared at his face in the mirror and concentrated with all his might. In the beginning, nothing had happened. Now and then he had managed a glimmer of a tint to his hair or a hint of color in his cheeks—nothing like the wild, uncontrollable changes that had taken over his whole body in the Deep Dark. He might have quit trying entirely except that Cole told him that when he was sleeping, sometimes his ears went pointy or his toes blended in with the bedsheets. This news had made Tinn equal parts excited and nervous.

His mother had allowed him to visit the goblins a handful of times during the summer, and with Kull's help, Tinn had twice managed to make his face go all green, but it had been like flexing a weak muscle. The moment he stopped concentrating, he went back to looking like himself.

The upside had been that, in the absence of any noticeable magic, his life had been able to remain more or less the same. He had been able to walk down the street with his family and start school in the fall like nothing had changed.

Except that it *had* changed.

Something inside him had shifted, and he couldn't put it back. After thirteen years of neighbors whispering about a monster hiding among them, Tinn's secret was about to become everybody's news. His breath came in shallow gulps. Evie was going to find out. He would give anything not to let Evie find out.

He lifted his head. The prickling feeling had stopped. Maybe it was over. Tinn glanced down at his hands. The left was its usual pale pink, but the right was now so dark it didn't even look real. It looked like a hand-shaped hole in the universe. He felt ill.

The back door of the schoolhouse opened, and Tinn stuffed both hands into his lap and tried to make himself as small as possible. Footsteps neared the shed. They paused.

Please be Cole. Please be Cole.

"Tinn?" It was Evie Warner.

Tinn's stomach attempted to fold itself gracelessly into a paper butterfly.

"Oh." Tinn's mouth was bone-dry. "Hi."

Evie pushed past the tall grass and squeezed in behind the shed.

"Don't come over. I'm . . . I'm sick. You'll catch it."

"No, you're not," said Evie.

Tinn swallowed. "I might be." With the way his stomach was churning, it was only half a lie. He put his head between his knees.

"It's okay," said Evie.

"It's really not," said Tinn. "You don't understand."

"That's true." Evie was quiet for a few seconds. "Do you

remember last year, when I was new? Do you remember the first time we talked back here?"

Tinn took a deep breath. "Egg toss," he said.

"Egg toss," agreed Evie.

"We lost," said Tinn.

"We played," she said. "You played. With me."

"You didn't want to play at all."

"I know." Evie kicked a dirt clod. "Rosalie Richmond kept calling me *gnome* and everybody was laughing. It was just like my old school all over again. So I was hiding." She scooted closer along the bricks. "But then you came to talk to me—even though I told you not to. Because you didn't understand."

"Rosalie's a jerk to everyone."

"That's what you said then, too. She made me feel like nobody. But you made me feel like . . . *somebody* again."

Tinn raised his chin. "Everybody's somebody."

"And you also told me I was *lucky*. I've been called a lot of things, but I think you're the first person to call me *lucky*. You said that when people call me names, at least I know it isn't true. You said at least *I* know who I really am."

Tinn nodded. He remembered stumbling over his words a lot more than that when he said it, but he was glad it had gotten through.

"And then you told me about . . . the stories."

Tinn cringed. "I should've kept my mouth shut. You were the only kid who didn't call me and Cole *goblin*."

"I'm glad you told me," she said. "Sometimes you gotta toss the egg and trust the other person is gonna do their best to catch it."

"We *lost* at egg toss," Tinn reminded her.

"No," said Evie, "we didn't."

They stared at their own feet for several moments.

"I saw it," Evie said at last. "Your hand."

Tinn felt all sweaty in spite of the cold bricks on his back.

"Is it . . . magic?" she asked.

"I guess?" Tinn closed his eyes and let the back of his head clunk against the wall. "Yeah. It is."

"So, it's you, then? You're the one who . . . you're the . . . the G word?"

Tinn nodded wretchedly.

"Can I see it?"

Tinn opened his eyes a crack to peek at Evie. She had gotten even closer. She didn't look particularly horrified or disgusted.

Slowly, he raised his hands.

"That's so neat," she said, leaning in closer. Then she caught herself. "I mean, not *neat*. It's fine. It's not a big deal."

"It's weird," said Tinn.

43

Evie held his ink-black hand in hers. "Yeah," she said. "It is weird." Her fingers laced between his.

The paper butterfly in Tinn's stomach burst into flames.

They sat behind the school, hand in hand, staring at the back of the dusty storage shed and saying nothing for a long time. Evie finally broke the silence. "My dad got a new job."

"Yeah?"

"He's working for Mr. Hill. They keep going out really early and taking samples."

"Samples of what?"

"I dunno. Dirt and rocks and stuff. It all seems pretty dumb. It's nice to see Dad excited, though. He's been all mopey and grumpy since he got fired. He and Mom keep fighting, too. She said she needed to go help my aunt in Glanville for a little while, but it's obvious she just wanted to get away."

Tinn nodded. "Sorry."

"It's okay. Things are getting better, at least. And hanging out with Uncle Jim has been fun. He doesn't baby me as much as everybody else does."

"I still can't believe you're related to Old Jim. Is the inside of his house full of creepy traps and animal heads and things?"

"Yes. It's amazing."

"I knew it."

Tinn's heart had gradually ceased pounding against his chest, and his head wasn't spinning anymore.

"Hey," said Evie. "Your hand."

Tinn looked down. "Huh." The usual color had returned to his skin, with the exception of a small, smeary ink stain across two fingers. He rubbed his palm and flexed his fingers experimentally. They felt normal.

"Can you change like that on purpose?" Evie asked.

"No. Well, sometimes. Not very well. I'm learning. It's all really new. I guess I just got a little anxious in there."

"Think you can make it to the end of class without freaking out again? If you want, I can tell everybody that you just barfed all over yourself and it was completely disgusting and embarrassing and you ran home mortified."

"That's really nice of you," said Tinn. "I think I'll be okay, though. I just need to stay calm."

"TINN!"

Evie and Tinn both jumped as a third face inserted itself into the gap between the buildings. The owner of the face wore an expansive smile, a smudge of dirt on her chin, and a mess of dark curls atop her head.

"Fable?" Tinn said. "How? What are you—"

"Oh my gosh, Tinn!" Fable said, bobbing up and down on her heels in her excitement. "Human places are a-MAZ-ing. There's a house up the road for horses, and I saw a door with a fancy, stripy pole that turned out to be a whole room for cutting hair. Isn't that funny? There's even a tiny little building just for pooping! Wanna see?"

"Um."

"Ooh! Is this your friend?" Fable directed her wide eyes to Evie. "You're pretty! My name's Fable. I'm Tinn's friend, too. Best friends. Forever. What's your name? Hey—we're both wearing dresses! That's fun! Tinn's mom sewed mine. Does your dress have the buttons in the back? Annie says they're kept back there because it looks nicer, but I wish they were in front because I like to look at the buttons. Mine's also got a bow on it that isn't even tied to anything. See? It just sits there." She turned and shuffled herself backward between the buildings to show off her bow.

"I'm Evie," said Evie. "Your dress is beautiful."

"Fable," Tinn managed finally, "what are you doing here? I mean. It's great to see you. But does your mom know you're in Endsborough? Is she . . . here?"

"Blurg. No. She dropped me off at your house again, but there was nobody home, so I came to find you."

"Well, yeah. It's a weekday. We're in school."

"This is school?" Fable looked dubiously at the dusty walls. "I thought school would be bigger."

"Well, no. I mean—school is inside. We're supposed to be in there right now."

"Oh my gosh. Yes," said Fable. "That sounds amazing. Let's do school!"

And without any further discussion, she whipped open the back door and strode inside the schoolhouse.

Tinn opened his mouth and shut it again.

"She seems nice," said Evie.

FOUR

"Could i please just go and check on Tinn?" Cole pleaded for the third time.

"For goodness' sake, Mr. Burton, sit down," Mrs. Silva chided. "Your brother does not need your help using the facilities. He's only in the little boys' room—he hasn't fallen out of the world."

Maybe not this time, Cole thought, but falling out of the world was an unpleasantly real possibility with Tinn.

He had made up his mind to leave anyway the moment Mrs. Silva's back was turned, but before his chance arrived, the door banged and the whole class craned their necks to see a new girl sauntering in.

"Oh!" Mrs. Silva said. "Hello, young lady."

"Hi!" said Fable. "Is this school? I'm here to do school."

Mrs. Silva faltered. "Er. Yes, my dear. This is school. Are you new to Endsborough?"

"Really new." Fable nodded. "I already found the horse house and the hair house, though. And the pooping house," she added with a snort.

"Fable?" Cole stood up.

"Cole!" Fable beamed. "You're doing school, too?"

"Do you know this person, Mr. Burton?" Mrs. Silva said.

"Yeah," he said. "She's a—a family friend. She's just visiting my mom."

"I see. Will she be staying long?"

"No," said Cole.

"Yes," said Fable.

"I see. Well, it's nice to meet you, Miss—I'm sorry, what was your surname?"

"Oh, I don't have a sir name," said Fable. "I'm a girl."

"Young lady," Mrs. Silva said. "I'm afraid I don't have any paperwork for your transfer. I'll need to make a note to speak to your parents. Tell me, what was your previous institution for learning?"

"What's a *previous instant toot-toot*?" said Fable.

"Your *education*," Mrs. Silva said, "prior to Endsborough?"

"Oh, I've learned lots of stuff. Let's see, I already know the math and most of the words. What else is there . . . oh— what's the one about which mushrooms make you get better and which ones make you dead?"

"I mean *where* were you educated? Your last *school*?"

"I do not understand the question," said Fable.

The door banged again and Tinn and Evie stumbled in. "New Fiddleham," said Tinn, hastily. "She's our cousin. From New Fiddleham. She's visiting."

Mrs. Silva raised an eyebrow. "Your brother just informed us that she was a family friend."

Tinn glanced at Cole. "Oh. Yeah. She is. She's a friend."

"Who is also family," added Cole. "She's a friend who is family. A family friend. That's exactly what I meant."

Fable grinned broadly at them both. "Aww. You guys."

Mrs. Silva's eye twitched in that special way it only seemed to twitch when Tinn and Cole were involved. "Well, I'm sure we can sort it all out at the end of the class. We have had enough disruption for one morning, I think. If you could all find your seats. Fable, is it? Why don't you sit right there for now, dear. The class was just about to put away their English workbooks and move on to mathematics. Have you any experience with algebra?"

"Not yet, but Annie Burton told me all about them. I'll probably get to wear one when I'm older."

Mrs. Silva blinked. Students around her giggled.

"Just . . . try to follow along with the other students," Mrs. Silva said. "Everyone take out a blank sheet of paper, please. Hana, will you kindly lend Fable a piece of paper?"

Twenty minutes later, Evie had successfully solved for x (which was seven), Cole had accidentally solved for three (which, it turned out, was still three), Tinn had managed to avoid changing colors even a little bit, and Fable had learned how to use a dip pen, gotten ink on both elbows and one eyebrow, and drawn a startlingly accurate cross section of an *Amanita* mushroom (*mycology*, incidentally, is the name for knowing which mushrooms make you get better and which ones make you dead, and even her mother would have had to admit that Fable had been a decent study at that).

Mrs. Silva was beginning to hold out a tenuous hope that she just might make it to lunchtime without another catastrophic disruption. She was wrong, of course, but hope is such a precious thing, one cannot really hold it against the woman for clinging to it. In the children's defense, the thunderous *BOOM* that shook Endsborough and sent the entire class hurrying to the shuddering windows to watch a cloud of smoke and dust rise over the tops of the buildings was not the slightest bit their fault.

FIVE

"DON'T LOOK AT ME LIKE THAT," THE QUEEN
said. "If you want the blackberry, you're going to have to
get it yourself."

The hedgehog made a squeaky, whiffling grunt at her
feet.

"I get enough of that tone from my daughter, thank you
very much. You have a stomach now. If you don't want to
be hungry, you'd better learn how to fill it."

Squidge shuffled about on the forest floor before balancing unsteadily on two fluffy hind legs as she tried to
pull the elusive fruit a little closer. The vine bobbed, and
Squidge rolled over backward in a spiny ball. The queen

was uncertain if the creature's clumsiness was a side effect of having spent the first half of her life as a pinecone or if hedgehogs were just like that.

Raina watched as the scruffy thing righted itself and made another attempt to reach the berry. She tried not to let herself think about how much raw magic it would take to *make* Squidge. The queen could communicate with a plant. She could even coax a plant to grow in the shape of an animal. But to make a plant *into* an animal? You could not simply make the world be what you wanted it to be. That was not how the world worked.

Squidge mewled mournfully as she tumbled onto her back for what must have been the dozenth time.

The queen rolled her eyes. "You *will* need to learn how to be yourself, sooner or later," she said, and finally bent the branch. Squidge brightened at once and pounced on the berry with glee. "And so will Fable," the queen sighed.

The sun cut through the canopy and birds sang loudly as the queen paced through the Wild Wood. A swarm of brownies was nattering in the thistles nearby. She let her feet carry her for several minutes without a destination in mind. This was her forest. It had been her mother's before her, and so it would be Fable's in turn.

Light danced off the tree trunks ahead in glittering waves. The queen glanced up. She swallowed. Just past a curtain of leaves, the pond awaited. She had not meant to come here—but here she was.

The spring was crystal clear, as always, its surface rippling gently in the breeze. A wispy willow stretched its limbs over the water on the far side. There, in the opposite corner of the pool, tucked in the shadow of the tree, a pair of emerald eyes shone.

"Hello, Kallra," said the queen.

The girl's face rose, droplets of water running down blue-green cheeks. She looked no older than Fable, but the queen knew better.

"It's good to see you, old friend," said the queen. "I could use some reassuring right about now."

Kallra turned her head ever so slightly to one side. Her skin glistened.

"I think," the queen went on, "that I might need to look forward."

Kallra nodded solemnly, and began to slip back under the surface.

"It's about Fable—"

But before she could finish, the girl had vanished. The queen stepped to the edge of the pond and peered in.

For several moments there was nothing but the chirping of birds and the hum of insects. Gradually, the ripples faded and the water's surface became like mirrored glass.

And there she was. The queen stared at the image as it coalesced. Her daughter's hair was its usual mess, and she was wearing the dress that Annie Burton had made for her. It was Fable, no mistake—except that everything was wrong.

The queen's breath caught in her throat.

Her daughter's cheeks and clothes were covered in ashes and caked in something darkly red. Her hazel eyes, usually so bright and full of mischief, were hollow, haunted, and streaming with heavy tears. As the queen looked on, Fable's lips parted in a wretched scream.

BOOM!

The crash was distant—miles away, perhaps—but it echoed around the hills and set a handful of birds fluttering and squawking from their perches.

The queen's eyes flicked toward Endsborough. Dust and smoke were rising from somewhere on the edge of town. Nowhere near the Burtons', she reassured herself, but her heart was racing.

She looked back to the pool. The horrible vision of Fable had vanished. Her own reflection was all that stared back at her now, worry etched in her brow like deep runes. The surface stirred as Kallra slowly rose.

The queen swallowed. "What was that?" she said. "What did you just show me? What's going to happen?"

Kallra pursed her lips.

"Please."

For a long moment, Kallra said nothing. The spirit of the spring owed her gifts to no one, and the queen knew it. The spirit's emerald eyes watched the queen with aching pity for several seconds—and then she drew a deep, slow breath. When she spoke, it was in a soft whisper, as silky as a stream trickling over river rocks.

"Your daughter's reign I have foreseen,
a broken and unready queen.
Crowned by blood and burning grass,
and a single shot of lead and brass."

Kallra delivered each word delicately, as if they were shards of glass that cut her tongue as she spoke them. As soon as she was done, the spirit slid away again, sinking remorsefully beneath the surface of the pool.

The queen watched numbly as a graceful blue-green bullfrog dove down under the water until it burrowed itself into the mud at the bottom of the pond.

A dull, cold lump was growing in her chest. "That, old friend," she managed, "was *not* reassuring."

SIX

THE AIR WAS STILL THICK WITH DUST AND smoke as the children crowded in to join the throng of townsfolk ogling the destruction. The inn at the forest's edge was missing a wall, and the plume of dark smoke rose high into the air.

"Whoa!" Tinn was standing on his toes to peer over the shoulders of the milling crowd. Mrs. Silva had given up trying to order the children back inside the school two blocks back, but she insisted they stay a safe distance from the accident.

"What do you see?" asked Evie.

"The wood along this side of the inn is all broken and twisted up," said Tinn. "Crazy. It's like the whole side of the building was a piece of chewing gum and it popped. Let's try to get closer."

"The people village is even more exciting than I imagined," Fable whispered as they squeezed in between the adults. "Can all the buildings do that?"

"I sure hope not," said Cole.

The inn's groundskeeper was relating his story for the fifth time as they emerged at the front of the group. "Scared me half to death," the man said. "The whole side of the building just threw itself at me while I was pruning. Grazed my knee real bad, but I dove out of the way in the nick of time."

"Any casualties, Burt?" somebody asked.

"Only my rhododendrons," he said. "Gloria got a group of volunteers together right away to check all the rooms. Looks like everyone got out okay. Fella in number nine got the worst of it, I think, but he was walkin' and talkin' when they hauled him out."

"Evie? Boys?" The kids turned at the sound of Annie's voice. "What on earth are you doing here—Fable?"

"Hi, Annie Burton!" said Fable. "I did school today!"

Annie shook her head and sighed. "Well, it's dangerous here, so stay with me, all of you. Don't get any closer."

"Dad!" Evie yelled and took off across the dusty street.

"Wait!" called Tinn and hurried after her.

"What did I *just* say?" Annie took a deep breath and marched after them.

Oliver Warner stood on the sidewalk in front of the inn. Beside him was seated a hunched figure—the former occupant of the ill-fated room number nine.

"Isn't that Mr. Hill?" said Tinn as they neared.

Jacob Hill was swaying and coughing as Mr. Warner put a hand on his shoulder to steady him. He wore the same tweed waistcoat and matching trousers, but they were now coated in plaster dust and had the sort of look that linen has after it has been crumpled into a ball. He rubbed his head and took slow breaths.

"Dad! What happened?" said Evie.

Her father's eyes widened. "Evie! Why aren't you in school right now?"

Hill glanced up. "Oh, I don't expect anybody is too worried about truancy right now," he wheezed. "Hi, kid. Come to see your dad be a hero?"

Evie looked skeptical. "*My* dad?"

"I didn't do anything special," Oliver said.

Hill nodded. "Pulled me out of the burning wreckage himself."

"Are you okay?" said Cole.

"I'll be fine." Hill looked for a moment like he was considering standing up, but then seemed to think better of it and remained on solid ground. "They'll have to try harder than that to see the last of Jacob Hill."

"You think someone did this on purpose?" said Tinn.

"It wouldn't be the first time somebody tried to sabotage me," Hill said. "It's okay. Really, it's good. Surest sign you're on your way to something great is somebody trying to get in your way." He chuckled weakly and set himself to coughing again.

"It's true," Mr. Warner said. "Tools have gone missing during the night and equipment has gotten moved around. Can't imagine why someone would want to mess with the operation, but there it is. A couple of days ago Lambert and Stokes said they were dead sure somebody was watching them from the forest, too. Gave Lambert the willies."

Hill nodded. "Spies."

"Hold on," Annie said. "You're surveying in the Wild Wood?"

Fable's eyes narrowed a fraction. She might not know what *surveying* meant, but she didn't like the idea of anybody doing it to her forest.

"No, no, of course not. I haven't got the permits to drill on government land," Hill said. "I bought seven acres of overgrown farmland right along the northwest edge of the forest, though."

"The old Roberson place," said Oliver.

"That's right," said Hill. "I hired a geologist who likes the odds that there could be a big oil reservoir hiding right under the Roberson Hills. We've been clearing land all week for a halfway decent drill site. It's been slow going even without saboteurs. Who knows what criminal element is lurking beyond the tree line, hiding in the forest like some rotten Robin Hood."

"You do know Robin Hood is the good guy in that story, right?" said Cole.

Fable scowled. "*Nobody* is supposed to be in the forest. Outsiders aren't allowed."

Hill shrugged. "Nobody is *supposed* to set off dynamite in an occupied building, either. Those scofflaws don't seem to care what they're allowed."

Tinn took a few tentative steps closer to the ruined building, stepping over bits of plaster and brick. The wood was splintered outward as if a freight train had erupted directly from room nine. He squinted up at the wreckage. "Huh," he said. "Are you sure there was an explosion here?"

"Of course there was an explosion," Mr. Warner said. "You're standing in the aftermath, kid."

Tinn scrunched up his face, unsatisfied. "It doesn't look like an explosion."

"Don't get so close," his mother chided him.

"What exactly happened in there?" Cole asked.

Hill shook his head. "I don't really know. Last thing I remember I was sorting through some soil samples we took yesterday, and then—it's all sort of a blur. Everything was loud and I was dizzy and . . . and then Oliver here was pulling a table off of me.

"What makes you think it wasn't an explosion, young man?" asked Hill.

Tinn pointed to the gaping hole in the wall. "It's just that the wood and bricks are all smashed outward, but there's no blast marks on the walls. I've seen the rocks after the miners do a big blast, and it always leaves a lot of marks, plus a certain smell. This just smells like a fireplace."

"Young man." Hill sat up, peering back into the wreckage. "If not an explosion, what do you think is capable of causing destruction like this?"

Tinn shook his head. "I have no idea."

"I can think of a few things," said a gruff voice from the crowd. Old Jim Warner stumped forward. "Kid's right. I've lived beside the Wild Wood long enough to recognize when something ain't normal. An' this?" He gestured to what was left of the inn. "This ain't normal."

"Oh, I wasn't saying anything about the Wild Wood," Tinn said.

"You should be," Old Jim grunted. "There's something goin' on here. Something . . . *magic*."

Hill laughed. When nobody else joined him, he stopped. "Wait. Really?" He looked around the faces of the assembly. "Magic? Is he serious right now?"

There were murmurs of anxious agreement from the crowd. Old Jim just let his dark gaze drift to the forest.

Fable did not like the glint in the old man's eyes.

SEVEN

Deep inside the wild wood sat a quiet, moss-covered cabin. The forest had all but claimed the little house. Sweet grasses grew from its rooftop and a fourth generation of swifts was chirruping in its chimney. Lichen grew on its ledges and ivy in its eaves. A goblin stood on its front step.

Chief Nudd took a deep breath.

Nudd was many things. He was a goblin, of course, and High Chief of the Hollowcliff Horde. He was Ambassador to the Elflands, Enforcer of the Goblish-Spriggan Alliance, Tiddlywinks Champion, and even an honorary deputy in New Fiddleham's human police department—or, at least,

Commissioner Marlowe had not yet tracked him down to take the badge back, and Nudd was not going out of his way to surrender it. What Nudd was *not* was satisfied.

The cabin brought back memories. Even though it was covered in vines and thick moss, Nudd could still recognize his own handiwork. The roof had held up well against the years, he noted with some pride. Nudd ran a hand along the weathered wood of the front step. The last time he had been to this place, his father—the old chief—had still been alive. And so had the woman.

She had been their fault, that woman in the woods. Under his father's rule, the horde had stolen the woman's baby and left a changeling in her place. It was tradition. The changeling would return in three days' time, and the child would lead a good life with the fairies, or so the old chief had told Nudd. It was not cruel, he insisted, it was simply the way things were done. It was what they trained for. What they had *not* trained for, however, was the woman. She had caught the fleeing goblin changeling before it ever reached the horde.

She forced the little creature to take her to the place in the woods where the fairies had come for her daughter. It was a quiet clearing, just west of the Oddmire. By the time they arrived, there was nothing to find but scuffed moss and a mound in the earth. Her daughter was long gone.

Day after day, the woman returned to that spot, crying out for the fair folk, the animals, the trees themselves to give her baby back. The fairies never came, and the forest never answered. The townsfolk did nothing to help, either. Other humans from the village paid her no mind, except to call her mad. She ignored them, and in time she left them all behind and made her home in the woods—waiting, searching, hoping beyond hope.

And that was where Nudd had found her.

She had built a drafty hovel facing the mound—staring at the gate she could never open. Nudd had watched from the woods as she went about her day, tending to a meager garden and weaving reeds into lopsided mats. Every so often she would freeze, gazing out into the forest, and she would speak one word to the wind. "Raina?"

Nudd's chest had grown heavy as he watched, and he soon realized that he owed the woman more than he could pay. Goblins do not abide red in their ledgers. Unpaid dues, to a goblin, are like a creeping itch. The horde had always justified child-stealing as a temporary debt. When the fairies took possession of the baby from the goblins, they took with it the guilt and the responsibility for its theft. This absolved the goblins. The fae, for their part, refused to take a child who was missed, which kept their conscience clear, as well—that was the entire purpose of the changeling, to keep the child from being missed, for at least as long as was required to complete the transaction. At the time, it had all sounded neat and tidy to Nudd.

Now that he saw the woman's face, he did not find it neat or tidy.

One morning, the woman awoke to find her firewood chopped and stacked. Nudd had watched silently from the bushes as she turned from the woodpile to the forest, scowling.

"This is not enough," she had declared, angrily.

The next day, her meager home had been transformed into a fine cottage. She emerged, startled, through a carved oak door that had not been there the night before, and walked around the cottage twice before she turned and glared at the forest again.

"This," she had called into the trees, "is not enough."

On the third day, she had found every cup, saucer, drawer, and boot in her house overflowing with coins—silver and gold and strange metals she had never seen before with inscriptions in languages she did not recognize. They could have bought her a castle. She stepped outside, and this time Nudd could have sworn she had looked straight at him as she glared into the forest.

"This is not enough."

And so, on the fourth morning, the woman had opened

her door to find Nudd himself on her front step. They had stared at each other until the goblin finally spoke.

"I canna get yer kin back," he had told her honestly. "What would ya have in her stead? Iffin I can deliver it, it will be yours."

She had stared down at the goblin for several long minutes. Nudd felt the pressure of her gaze, but he was the son of a chief, and so he did not bow or lower his eyes. Finally, she spoke. "A promise," she said. "Never again. Never let another mother find one of your kind where her baby should be. Never let another child wake to find its world stolen away. Never. Not once. Promise me."

Nudd had stood in silence for another long time before nodding. "I promise." His father had been the chief to bring their horde to this bold new world. Nudd would be the chief who brought the world a bold new horde.

He had kept his promise. That fool Kull had almost broken it thirteen years ago when he attempted to steal the Burton boy—but it had all worked out in the end.

Now Nudd's ears perked up, and he drew himself out of his memories back to the present. The air around the cottage was cool and smelled of lemongrass and damp earth. Bugs buzzed and leaves shuffled in the breeze above him—and there was something else. "Hm. I didn'a think ya came here anymore," he said to the shadows.

The queen stepped into the sunlight. She was a fine witch, Nudd thought. Very like her mother, indeed. "I did not think I needed an invitation," she said. "What are *you* doing here?"

"Gettin' old." Nudd shrugged. "Would ya rather I go?"

She hesitated. "No," said the queen. "Stay." With a deep breath, she sat beside the chief on the mossy front step.

Nudd's eyebrows rose, but he said nothing.

"This is where she died," she said. Her voice was hollow.

Nudd nodded. "Aye," he said. "But it's also where she lived."

Birds tweeted and the shadows of a low cloud rolled across the grass. "Do you think she would be upset," the queen asked softly, "that I've just let the forest have it?"

"The house? Oh, lass." Nudd clucked.

"Don't call me lass."

"Raina. Aside from her baby girl, this forest is the only thing yer mother ever loved. First Witch o' the Wood, she was. First Queen o' the Deep Dark. She gave her bones ta this forest—she certainly wouldn't care if it took a pile of old lumber, too. She'd only be upset that she never got ta see what a fine queen her daughter turned out ta be."

The queen said nothing.

"Or what a fine one her granddaughter is going ta become," Nudd added.

The queen sighed. "I fear that transition may be a difficult one."

Nudd frowned. "Well. All transitions are—"

"I've spoken to Kallra."

Nudd put a hand to his brow. "Otch! No wonder yer so sour today! Never go in for prophecies, myself—what sort of fool asks a fortune teller about her own death? Are ye new, queenie? Thought ya had more sense than that!"

"I did not ask about my own death. I asked about Fable becoming queen."

"Same thing, innit?"

The queen sagged. "It is possible I have been a fool."

"Well." Nudd softened and gave her a sympathetic half smile. "What's done is done. Let's have it—what did the slippery spirit tell ya?"

She recited the prophecy numbly.

"A *single shot of lead and brass*, eh?" Nudd took a deep, bracing breath. "Bullet, then? That's na so bad, as deaths go."

The queen raised a skeptical brow.

"There's an end comin' fer us all, Raina. No use frettin' over it. Yer bullet is likely a very long way off. Loads o' time, yet. Ye'll be a proper old hag by the time it finds ya."

The queen nodded. In the back of her mind, however, she could not help but recall that the face she had seen in that pond—her daughter's face, caked in soot and blood and flowing tears—had still been so young.

"And if Fable isn't ready when the time comes? What then?"

"Well, of course she won't be ready. Were *you*? Ya think *I* was ready ta be chief when my father died? Been at it fer ages now, and I'm still barely ready most mornings. We're never ready until we need ta be. Yer gonna have ta get used to the idea that ya won't ever see Fable become the queen she's meant ta be. That's just how it works. I'm sorry, Raina. Just gotta do yer best by her until then. She'll be all right, though. Iffin it makes ya feel any better, I'll keep an eye on her. Just like I've kept an eye on you."

The queen nodded. "Just how long do goblins live, exactly?" she asked.

Nudd smiled and leaned back against the soft wood. "Long enough," he said, "ta pay our debts."

EIGHT

"I THINK IT MIGHT BE BEST IF WE TAKE FABLE home," Annie said as they made their way back up the dusty street and away from the milling crowd. People had already begun dispersing by the time the town's entire police force—all five officers—had arrived to help control the chaos.

"Aw—but I just got here," said Fable.

"And I'm sure your mother will be worried sick. Does she even know you're in town?"

"Yes. Of course she knows. Obviously. Sort of."

"That's very reassuring. You're going home."

"Aww. But I was doing really good. I went to school. And not just the outside part where Tinn was hiding—I went inside and did writing and numbers and everything. My picture was the best one of the whole class."

"Nobody else was drawing pictures," said Cole.

"Hold on," said Annie. "Why was Tinn hiding?"

Fable shrugged. "People hide sometimes. I know a guy who's really good at hiding. He looks just like tree bark, so he can hide right in front of your face. Also, he's a lizard. He lives in the forest. I'm a pretty good hider, too. Wanna see me hide somewhere?"

"Please don't, sweetie. Would you give us just a moment? Boys, family chat."

Fable rocked on her heels while the Burtons stepped to the side of the road for a private conversation.

"Did Mrs. Burton say they're taking you home?" Evie said. "Like, all the way back to New Fiddleham?"

"Where? Oh! Ha, ha. No. I don't really live there," said Fable. "That's just our special made-up story that I'm supposed to tell people if they ask me about it. It's a lie, but Annie says it's the good kind of lie that's okay because it doesn't hurt anybody, and because people won't really believe that I'm from the Wild Wood anyway. I'm getting really good at lying. Wanna hear me do it?"

Evie blinked. "You're from the Wild Wood?"

"I am *not* from the Wild Wood," said Fable.

Evie stared at her. "What?"

"Pretty good, right?" said Fable, proudly. "I used to have a hard time with lying, but I'm way better now. You totally believed me."

"Right," said Evie. "But really you *are* from the Wild Wood?"

"Yeah. Me and my mama. She's the Queen of the Deep Dark. Tinn and Cole say she's famous or something."

Evie stared. "Yeah," she said. "Right. Your mom's the Queen of the Deep Dark, Witch of the Wild Wood, Mother of Monsters?"

"Yup," said Fable, kicking a bit of cracked brick across the road. "I mean . . . that last one's not my favorite, but that's her."

"No way. Prove it," said Evie. "Do something witchy."

"What's witchy?"

"I don't know. Something magical."

Fable considered. "Hmm. I'm not supposed to turn into a bear around people, and I'm not good at my mama's sort of magic yet."

"Did you say a bear?"

"Ooh! I could do slappy sparks. That one's easy. Your hair's not super flammable, is it?"

"Just regular flammable, I think."

Fable spread her hands wide and then clapped once, hard. A shower of sparks tumbled from between her palms for just an instant, as if from a welder's torch. Evie jumped.

"It's better at night," said Fable.

Evie's eyes went wide. She glanced up and down the street, but nobody appeared to be looking their way. "Holy heck!" she whispered. "That's amazing!"

Fable nodded, grinning. Her mother usually scolded her for slappy sparks. "Right? It *is* amazing. Thank you."

Across the street, Annie furrowed her brow. "You changed?" she whispered. "In the middle of class?"

"I didn't mean to," said Tinn. "It just sorta happened."

"Nobody saw," said Cole.

"I knew it was a bad idea to let you keep testing your powers. You shouldn't be messing with magic."

"It's no big deal, Mom," Tinn said. "Really."

"I'm canceling this weekend," she said. "I should never have agreed to an overnight in the first place. You probably shouldn't be going to the cliffs at all."

"What? No! Please, Mom," Tinn said. "I need to learn how to control it. That's the whole point." He looked to Cole for support, but his brother shrugged.

"I don't know, Tinn," Cole said. "Maybe it's too much too soon. Maybe you should just be . . . *you*. For a little while. We could just be *us* again. Like normal."

Tinn shot his brother a betrayed look. "*Normal* isn't possible anymore! Neither of you understands. I need real practice with real goblins. If I don't know how it works, then I can't stop it from happening. Mom. Please."

Annie pursed her lips.

"You're sure nobody saw you?"

"Nobody," Tinn said. "Well. One body. Evie saw."

"What did you tell her?"

Tinn sucked in a breath through clenched teeth. "Oh. Just . . . you know . . . everything," he said. "It's fine, though. She's fine with it. Really. She understands."

Annie rubbed her face with one hand. "We practiced for this, kid." Tinn shuffled his feet. Annie sighed and composed herself. "You know I love you. And you know you have nothing to be ashamed of. It's just . . . dangerous. Even Fable understands that you can't just go telling people everything."

Across the street, Evie leaned in close to Fable. "I want to know *everything*."

"Okeydokey," said Fable.

"If your mom's a queen, does that mean you're a real-life princess?"

"Probably." Fable cocked her head. "Maybe. What's a princess?"

"You know, a *princess*. Like in stories."

"I think my mama told me different stories than yours did. Are princesses predators or prey?"

Evie leaned against a fence post and considered this. "Well, storybook princesses are always getting locked in dungeons or carried off by dragons. So . . . prey, I guess? Mostly they wear pretty dresses and get married to gallant knights."

"Hm. Pretty sure I'm not a princess, then. Well, maybe the part with the dragons could be fun."

"But your mom's a queen."

"Yeah. So?"

"So that means you'll be a queen someday, right?"

"I guess."

"I'm pretty sure that makes you a princess."

"Am not. Shut up. *You're* a princess."

"I wish," said Evie. "I'm not an anything." She picked at a splinter on the fence post.

"Of course you're a something! I bet you have all kinds of adventures! I bet you go walking down real streets wearing real shoes all the time, and buying things with money with faces on it, and saying stuff like, *How do you do, my good fellow. Cheerful porkpies to you.* I bet you even use umbrellas when it rains."

Evie giggled. "That isn't adventure stuff. That's just boring life."

"What's an adventure, then?"

"I don't know, maybe learning actual magic straight from the all-powerful Queen of the Deep Dark?"

"Blarg." Fable stuck out her tongue. "You want to get judged by stupid trees all day, you can be my guest."

Evie bit her lip.

"What?" said Fable.

"Could I, though?" she said. "Be your guest? I know absolutely everything there is to know about the Wild Wood already. I have three books about it. Well. One of them is just a book about forests, and the other two are journals that I filled with facts and stories that my uncle Jim told me. I would give anything to go on a completely real adventure in the Wild Wood, though."

Fable considered Evie.

Evie's eyebrows rose eagerly.

"Fine." Annie relented. "You can still visit the horde this weekend." Tinn pumped his fist in silent victory. "But you have to positively promise me you will be more careful. I mean it. You need to keep your secrets. But not from me. No secrets from me." She let out a puff of air. "Family secrets."

"I got it, Mom."

They made their way back across the street to where Evie and Fable were talking.

"Ahem. Hello, Evie," Annie said. "So, I understand you had an . . . informative day at school today?"

Evie smiled innocently.

"Evie's gonna come visit me in the forest," Fable blurted out. "And we're gonna find sprites and jump out of trees and I'm gonna try to teach her how to be a bear."

"Wow. Okay. Nope. None of that," said Annie. "Good Lord. Can *none* of you children remember anything we practiced?"

"It's okay, Mrs. Burton," Evie said. "I won't tell anybody about Tinn. Or about Fable. Nobody listens to me, anyway."

"Thank you very much, Evie."

It was then that Oliver Warner shuffled up the road toward them, and they said their goodbyes. Before they turned the corner, Evie glanced back behind her father and mimed locking her lips tight. Tinn flashed her a thumbs-up.

Annie and the boys accompanied Fable as far as the creek near the twins' old knotted climbing tree. Across the trickling stream, the forest waited patiently for Fable's return. She was no sooner on the opposite bank than a familiar cloak emerged from the shadows. The queen acknowledged Annie with the faintest nod before she and Fable melted back into darkness.

"It was the *best* day, Mama." Annie and the boys could hear Fable's voice through the underbrush. "I wore my new dress, and I saw a house just for pooping, and I did school, and a building exploded, and I made a new friend! Oh no! I forgot to ask if we're *forever* friends. I'm pretty sure we are, though. It feels like forever friends."

"Fable." They heard the queen sigh. "Fable, no."

NINE

"After I do my chores today, can I go back to the people village?"

"No."

The morning sun washed the glen with highlights of gold. Fable had been up already when the queen awoke, still buzzing from yesterday's adventure.

"Okay. *Before* I do my chores today, can I go back to the people village?"

The queen pursed her lips. "I should never have indulged this. No, Fable. The human world is not our world. It is not safe. Theirs is a world of unnatural machines.

They have traps and guns and"—her voice caught in her throat—"and bullets," she finished more quietly.

"Mama, you have no idea what the human world is!" said Fable. "You should've seen it! There's fancy buildings and fancy food and fancy *people*."

"I am well aware of the people," said the queen wearily.

"Why do you hate them so much?"

"I don't hate them. I just want them to stay on their side."

"Why do there have to be sides?"

"Because there *are*." The queen closed her eyes. "There *are* sides. You can't just make the world what you want it to be, Fable."

"Why not?"

The queen hesitated. It was not the question but the intensity in her daughter's voice that disarmed her. She squared her jaw. "Because you can't. Try letting the world make *you* what *you* need to be, instead."

Fable scowled, but did not argue any further.

"Listen, child. I'm glad you had a nice time with your friends," the queen said. "Really, I am. Of all the people in the whole wide world, you might have found the very best ones. But you went into town without my consent, and that sort of disobedience I cannot abide. This is serious, Fable. Endsborough is off-limits until I say otherwise. Understood?"

Fable rolled her eyes. "Understood."

"Thank you. Now, go finish your chores. The winds last night tangled up a lot of the southern witching knots, and they're not going to sort themselves out."

Fable grudgingly made her way off into the forest to tend to the wards.

The queen leaned against the trunk of a broad elm. The elm leaned in to meet her.

"She will be ready when she needs to be," the queen said aloud. The leaves rustled above her. "Me? I'm not sure I'll ever be ready."

The forest did not respond.

The queen felt an uncomfortable prickle running up her spine. She stiffened. Something was wrong.

The queen listened. All around her the wind whipped through the treetops a little too quickly, and the forest rang with a sudden jarring pain. It rippled through twisted roots and high branches. The queen cringed. Her stomach turned.

Before she knew what she was doing, the queen was running.

Her feet scarcely touched the forest floor. The woods bent around her and rushed past her on either side, drawing her forward. After several minutes, her lungs burned, but she hardly felt them. The ache in her bones was growing stronger as she neared the northwest corner of the woods, and she realized where the forest was pulling her—she was nearing one of the Grandmother Trees.

From the distance came a rhythmic screech of metal teeth on wood and the murmur of men's voices. The queen's blood was hot in her veins. *No. They would not dare.*

She slowed as the foliage around her thinned and the light of the sun cutting between tree trunks made her eyes ache. Palpable waves of distress rolled off the Grandmother Tree. Ahead of the queen lay a broad clearing. The edge of her domain. And the world of men.

"Clear out!" a voice yelled.

The queen lurched to a stop as a spasm shot through her like electricity.

"Here it comes! Warner—back up!"

The great, towering Grandmother Tree had begun to make an unsettling series of pops and groans. The queen was close enough now that she could see the men jogging away up the nearby hills, axes and long, wicked saws still clutched in their hands. She was too late.

Crack!

Numbly, she watched the ancient pillar tip forward.

There were more sickening snaps and pops, the wood shrieked, and then the whole thing came down with a deafening *CRUNCH.*

It was over.

The queen felt sick.

All around her, she could hear the quiet whimpers of the nymphs and the pixies. Their voices melted into a whispered dirge, and it made the queen's chest ache.

In the clearing, men began to laugh.

The queen's jaw shook. Her fists vibrated with fury as, above her, the sky grew cloudy and the wind blew cold.

"Whoo-ee. She nearly took your head off there, Oliver!" somebody shouted. The men were clapping one another on the back.

The queen's muscles tensed. *She's about to take all of your heads off,* she thought. Her pulse pounded in her ears. She could feel the vines beneath the soil waiting for her command. The air crackled with furious anticipation.

"You best be more careful," shouted another man. "I do not want to be the one to tell that little girl of yours her daddy's not coming home."

The queen froze.

"Good job, everyone. Let's get back to work, now! Stokes, you and Lambert get started on those branches. Be nice to get this thing stripped before those clouds open up."

The queen turned away. This she could not watch.

The winds died and the forest fell quiet. The queen drew slow, shuddering breaths as she stalked away. With each chuckle and boisterous hoot that followed her, echoing between the trees, she felt a hot ball of wrath rise again in her throat. With great force of will, she swallowed it back down again.

She became aware of many eyes peering at her through the leaves as she walked away. The faces of several grieving nymphs melted into the bark of the nearby trees, and a fluttering pixie light dimmed behind a low fern. A raspy voice drifted down from a mossy branch. *"She does nothing?"* it uttered in Spriggan.

"There are times when doing nothing is better than the alternative," the queen answered. She took great care to keep her voice measured and even. "Violence," she said, "is not strength."

The moss above her quivered. *"And nothing,"* the raspy voice answered, *"is not something."*

TEN

Salty air rippled across dry grasses as Annie, Cole, and Tinn approached the cliffs that evening. The voyage through the Wild Wood to the goblin horde had once seemed impossible, but the Burtons had now made the trip half a dozen times. It was no more than an hour's travel if they kept to the secret goblin path, which skirted around the worst of the forest's obstacles— and the protection the queen had granted them was enough to ward off most of the creatures who might wish them harm.

Chief Nudd met them at the mouth of the passage that led to the horde's cliffside village. Kull was at the chief's elbow, and a pair of sentries with drab green freckles and very sharp spears stood behind them.

Nudd greeted Annie with a tip of his coal-black top hat. "I trust the forest behaved herself." The bright plume of cardinal feathers danced in the ocean breeze. "Good ta see ya again, boys."

"It was fine," Annie replied. "There's some pink heather coming in along the stream. It's quite cheery, actually."

"That's grand. Mind ya dinna pick any. Brownies are thick this season, an' they likes ta nest in shrubs. Take yer finger right off if ya give 'em half a chance, little blighters. Ha, ha."

"Good to know," said Annie.

"Are you absolutely sure you want to spend the whole night here?" Cole whispered to Tinn. "You could just visit for the day, like last time."

"You know I'm sure," said Tinn. "I'd barely get started before it was time to walk home again."

Cole nodded, but he knew that if his brother were being honest, he'd admit he was anything but sure. Tinn was probably terrified. Cole certainly was. He could not remember a night he had slept without his brother right across from him. They had shared a bedroom, shared a tent, and even slept under the open stars together once or twice. It had always been the two of them against the world. But this was something Tinn had to do alone.

"Are *you* gonna be okay?" Tinn asked.

"Me?" said Cole. "I'm always okay. You know that." His voice was almost convincing. "I'm not the one who's gonna be sleeping in a drafty cave all night."

Cole would have gladly slept in a drafty cave if it meant he could be a part of this adventure with his brother; he would have slept in the mouth of an active volcano. But the goblins had made it abundantly clear that humans were permitted in the horde only under the most extenuating circumstances. The mere proximity of the humans as they dropped off Tinn each week had been rankling some of the more traditional goblins.

Cole tried to manage a cheeky smile as he socked his brother in the arm. "Don't get into too much trouble without me," he said.

Kull, who had been rocking back and forth with excitement from the moment the boys had crested the hill, finally shuffled forward. "Tinn! Got a new scroll picked out fer today. Goblish shanties. Dinna worry, I done transliterated it inta human, but I thought we could work on yer vocalizin'. Proper gnarls and howls are as much a part of goblin culture as eye gougin' or ferret stew."

For just a moment, Tinn glanced back, and Cole saw in his eyes the same Tinn who had dropped out of their school play after just a week of rehearsals because he was sure he would mess up his lines in front of an audience, the same Tinn who had crumpled up his geography project because he would have had to present it by himself at the science fair, the same Tinn who had never dared do anything, really, unless Cole had done it, too. If he really pressed Tinn right now, this was the moment Cole could talk his brother out of it. He took a deep breath.

"Well?" he said. "Go on. You're gonna be the best goblin ever." His smile very nearly reached his eyes.

"I'll tell you all about it when I get back," said Tinn. "Bye, Cole. Bye, Mom. Love you! I'll see you tomorrow!"

"Little does yer brother know," Kull was saying as he led Tinn down the narrow ledge along the face of the cliffs, "that the best goblin ever was Gripp Ap Mull back in the era of the Ratty Badger. I'll work a bit o' that inta our Goblish history lesson tomorrow mornin'."

Annie wrung her hands as she watched her son vanish around the curve of the cliffside.

"Yer lad's in good hands," Nudd assured her. "The whole of the horde will be lookin' out for him. When shall we be expectin' ya, then?"

"Tomorrow afternoon—no, wait. Early evening, actually, if it isn't too much trouble. It's just that I'll be starting a new job in the morning."

Cole looked down at his feet while they talked. He didn't want his mother to start a new job. Not so soon. Not on the same day Tinn was going to be gone. Cole would be left utterly alone in a silent, empty house all day. It made his stomach feel funny just thinking about it.

"Oh, aye?" Nudd said. "Good on ya. Humans have such fascinatin' careers. Whatcha workin' at? Fire brigade? Detective? What's the one with the lions and elephants in the big tent?"

"Nothing so exciting," Annie said. "Just stocking shelves in a shop. How does around six o'clock sound? Half past at the latest."

"No trouble at all. We're happy ta have the lad." Nudd gave a wave of his hand, and the sentries turned to follow Kull and Tinn down the narrow path.

Annie nodded. She put a hand on Cole's shoulder and took a steadying breath. "Let's go, big guy."

"Take good care of him," Cole called after the retreating chief.

"Always do," Nudd answered back. "Dinna worry about yer brother, lad. His trainin' has been goin' very well."

"It's going terribly," said Tinn.

He and Kull stood alone in the broad cave that served as their training room. A narrow opening to one end let in a fresh breeze and the sound of waves breaking against the rocks below.

"I still can't figure out how to control the transformations," Tinn went on. "My whole hand turned black as ink this time. And I couldn't make it stop. I almost blew my whole secret and showed the entire class that I'm a goblin."

"Ah." Kull nodded. "And that's . . . bad. Right."

"I don't get it. That never happens here with you. It never happens when I'm just practicing at home with Cole, either."

"Well, ya dinna have ta keep a secret in those places," Kull said. "Hard ta break a secret when yer na keepin' it."

Tinn leaned his back against the cave wall. "I just don't see why it has to be so hard for me. Do other changelings have this much trouble controlling their powers?"

Kull hopped up on a worn old stool and rubbed his splotchy head. "Other changelings are na you," he said. "Ya got ta understand, lad, most changelings dinna stay human more'n a few days. Once, in the era of the Manky Basilisk, a changelin' managed ta stay human fer a full fortnight.

They wrote all about it. It was a big deal. And after they come home—well—that's it. Most changelings dinna have any magic left after the first go-round. None of 'em have ever touched the fabric o' the universe fer a recharge the way you did. They get their big day, impersonate a child, and then they're back in the horde, just one o' the lot with nothin' ta set them apart except a fine story ta tell."

"What does that mean for me?" asked Tinn. He had been impersonating a child his whole life, although it had never felt like an impersonation before. He hadn't known how to be anything else. He was beginning to feel he didn't know how to be anything at all.

"It means yer unique," said Kull. "Ya gotta learn how ta be *you* an' stop worryin' about how ta be someone else."

"What if I'm never any good at changing?" Tinn asked. "I mean—I haven't gotten it right once. Not really right. What if I never do?"

Kull regarded him thoughtfully for a moment. "Hm. Ya see them lights?" Along the back wall was a line of messy wires hung with bright, glowing coils in glass tubes. Tinn had marveled at the electric lights on his first visit. Endsborough still relied on oil lamps, but Tinn had heard all about electricity from his classmate Hana Sakai, whose parents had taken her to Glanville for the fair last year. On his first visit, Tinn had asked Kull if he could touch one of the coils, and Kull had said, "Sure!" So Tinn had poked it, and the jolt had sent him tumbling backward across the floor. It had been hours before the feeling had fully returned to his arm. Goblin education looked different than human education.

"Rigged those lights up myself," Kull said. "I knew nothin' about electricity when I started. First time I turned 'em on, they didn'a do a thing. Hummed a bit is all. Made my tongue tingly when I gnawed on 'em. So, ya know what I did?"

Tinn shook his head.

"I adjusted. Tinkered with the couplin's, turned up the generator, added a bit more solder ta the connections. Second go-round, I blasted a burnt strip clear across the wall and gave three o' my neighbors heart attacks. I didn'a wake up fer days. Nudd tells me he had good money on me fer dead."

"Wait—you almost died? You let me poke those!"

"Oh, huck up. Yer fine. Point is: what do ya think I did as soon as I finally woke up?"

"Got medical attention?"

"I adjusted. And I tried again. And again. I learned more each time, see? I learned about fuses and dampeners and conductivity. Iffin it wasn'a fer all the times my plans didn'a go the way I wanted 'em to, we'd still be in the dark right now." Kull jabbed a stubby finger at Tinn. "Yer still sortin' out how ya work, boy. Yer learnin' what ya can do and who's inside ya. Dinna be afraid of a few sparks or a burnout from time to time. That's na failure. That's fine-tuning."

Tinn nodded. "I think I understand," he said. "Although gnawing on live wires probably isn't the best way to learn about power."

Kull waved his hand. "Bah," he said. "Ya know what they say. *Never learn nothin' iffin ya dinna gnaw on a few live wires.*"

"That is definitely not a thing that anybody says. That's a terrible idea, and it is probably going to kill you. I mean, point taken and all, but maybe don't do that."

Kull chuckled. "Shall we get to it, then? Straight ta transformation again, or maybe shanties first this time?"

Tinn took a deep breath. "Transformation," he said. "I'm ready to try some fine-tuning."

ELEVEN

FABLE HUGGED THE TREE TRUNK WITH ONE arm and let her feet dangle down from the high branch, feeling the tree sway lazily beneath her. The air was crisp, and leafy treetops rippled in the morning breeze. The sky was just waking up, still rimmed with gentle pinks, but it was growing brighter by the minute. From her pine tree vantage point, Fable could not yet see the rising sun over the tops of the forested hills, but she could see the house. She watched the house.

Her mother had been very clear about Fable not leaving the forest, so she hadn't. Endsborough was absolutely, positively out of bounds. Fable had become an expert in bending her mother's rules, finding loopholes and cutting the corners ever so slightly—but she knew better than to actually break any of them. Her mother had been grumpy about something all yesterday afternoon, but for once she did not seem to be grumpy about *Fable*—and Fable was happy to keep it that way for as long as possible.

There was movement behind one of the windows. Fable straightened. It might be nothing more than the Burtons' chubby cat again. Fable could see infuriatingly little from so far away. A distant *click*. Had that been the front door? Annie stepped into view, walking down the road toward town, wearing that pretty coat that came down to her knees, the one with the bright, shiny buttons. Apparently, dresses needed to hide their buttons in the back, but it was fine for coats to have them in the front.

"Good morning, Annie Burton!" Fable yelled. "Hello!" She waved broadly, and the tree swayed wildly with her movements.

Annie could not hear her. She continued to march on down the road until she vanished around the bend. Fable sagged. She had a clear view of the boys' window from where she perched—if only she could get their attention. She snapped a tiny pinecone from one of the scrawny branches above her, leaned as far back as she dared, and hurled it toward the house. It spun in the wind and came to land in a bush far below. It had not even reached the Burtons' back garden. Fable needed a better plan.

Five minutes later, she climbed back up to the top of the swaying pine tree with a pocketful of rocks. The first one she threw in a similar fashion, and it failed in a similar fashion. The next she held carefully in one hand. She cupped her palm loosely around it. She hooked a foot snugly around the branch below her, lifted her empty hand, and slapped it hard down atop the stone. A shower of sparks burst from between her fingers and the stone shot out from her hands like it had been fired from a miniature cannon. Fable flew backward. She would have fallen a very long way if not for her foothold. She hung upside down for a moment and grinned, then quickly righted herself. She had not seen exactly where the rock had landed, but she suspected it was somewhere near the vegetable patch. This could work.

She tried a second rock, and this one skipped off into the gravel on the side of the house. Closer! Sparks flew as a third shot assaulted the rosebushes, a fourth flew wide, and then the fifth finally made contact with the house.

It clattered along the rooftop and came to rest near the chimney. Fable let out a whoop and waited. Nothing happened.

She frowned. Another clap and another burst of sparks as Fable tried a sixth rock and then a seventh, really getting the hang of it by the eighth. The ninth might have had a bit more force than she really needed—it lodged itself with a solid *crack* in the wood of the back door—but still no Burton boys emerged.

That was when Fable smelled smoke. She glanced down. *Oh,* she thought. *Right. That's why Mama hates slappy sparks.*

By the time Cole made his way into the forest, the fire was already out. "Hey, Fable," he said, sliding over a mossy log. "Did you shoot my house?"

"You came!" Fable bounded across the slightly smoky forest floor and launched herself at Cole. She squinted at him for a second. "Just one of you?"

"Tinn's spending the day with his, um, *other* family," said Cole. "Did you light a signal fire just to get my attention?"

"Oh," said Fable. "That . . . is exactly what happened. Yes. I did that. On purpose. And you came!"

"Well, what do you need?"

Fable shrugged. "I dunno. What do *you* need?"

Cole shook his head. "Well. A friend to hang out with would be nice, I suppose," he said. "Wanna go exploring?"

Fable's eyes doubled in size and her fists shook. "SO MUCH!"

Cole laughed. "Okay, then. You've got soot on your cheek, you know."

"I know!" Fable said. "It's from all the stuff I lit on fire! I tried to put it out with my brain-hand, but that never works, so I had to use my hand-hands and a buncha wet dirt. Hey! Wanna go see if we can find any morning dew sprites before they're all gone?"

The two of them trooped along the grassy gully, up over clover-blanketed hills, and down along the shores of the Oddmire as the sun crawled its way over the eastern treetops.

"You have no idea how boring it is," Fable said, hopping up on a mossy stump, "practicing *proper* magic all the dang time. Hours."

"Are you kidding?" said Cole. "I would give anything to have magic like yours."

"Well, apparently it's not enough unless it's magic like *hers*. A good Witch of the Wood is supposed to be so *perfect*."

"At least you can do magic. Between all the stuff you can do and all the stuff Tinn can do, I'm starting to feel like I can't do anything at all."

"How's it going with Tinn, anyway?" asked Fable.

"It's—" Cole paused. "It's weird."

"Weird how?"

"Weird that Tinn has a whole long-lost family that isn't mine." They picked their way up an old, dry creek bed. "I mean—I'm happy for him. Really, I am. It's good that he's getting to know them. It's just . . ."

"Lonely?" said Fable. "Scary?"

Cole plopped down on a dusty boulder to catch his breath. "We both spent our whole lives being afraid to be the changeling. Now that I know it's him and not me—I mean . . . I never imagined I would feel . . . It's stupid."

"Feel what?"

"Jealous, I guess."

"You *want* to be a goblin?" Fable sat down on the bank across from him.

"No. It's not that." Cole rubbed his neck. "You know Kull? The one that's been taking care of Tinn when he visits the horde?"

"Yeah. My mama hates that guy pretty hard."

"Yeah. Well, I don't know exactly how parenting works for goblins—Tinn says there's something about an egg and a brood ceremony—but however it works, Kull has been acting kinda like, well, like a dad to Tinn. Kull's been able to answer a lot of questions for him." Cole shuffled his feet along the dry, cracked dirt. "With Mom starting up work now and Tinn gone all the time, it's just left me thinking more and more about . . ." Cole let the words trail off.

Fable nodded. She knew about Cole's father and about his disappearance back when the boys were still babies.

"You might find him someday," said Fable. "Mama says my dad died in a fairy war."

"Sorry," said Cole. "That's rough."

"Tell you what. I'll be your dad if you be mine," Fable offered, jumping to her feet.

Cole laughed.

"I bet I'd be a super good dad," said Fable. "What's something dads say?"

"I wouldn't know." Cole pushed himself up and rejoined Fable as she pressed on up the next hill.

"Me, neither," said Fable.

"How about advice?" suggested Cole. "Dads are supposed to teach you life lessons, right?" He cleared his throat. "Ahem. A penny saved is a penny earned, young lady."

"Nice!" said Fable. "I will treasure that advice forever, Father. What's a penny?"

"Now you do one," said Cole.

"Hm. Okay. Never offend a spriggan, young man, for their tempers are short and their grudges are long."

"That's good!" said Cole. "You're right, you do make a good dad. What's a spriggan?"

"What's a spriggan? How do you not know what a spriggan is? Jeez, no wonder your mom doesn't want you to wander around the woods on your own." They crested the next rise and Fable pointed toward a shimmering pond in a copse of trees just ahead. "Thirsty?" she asked.

Cole followed her. The forest buzzed with life, but the pool was calm and quiet.

"There's a freshwater spring under the surface," said Fable. "It comes up here, and then goes back underground again. It surfaces as a little stream down the hill a ways." She cupped her hands and took a big sip from the pond.

"Is it really okay to drink that water? Isn't it dirty?"

"Who do you think you're talking to? I know what I'm doing. This is only the cleanest water in the whole forest. Maybe the whole world."

"There's a frog swimming in it."

"What, her? That's just Kallra. She won't bother you. She's a girl sometimes. Besides, frogs swimming in a pond is the best way to know that the water is good. Don't you know anything?"

"Hold on. Back up. That's who?"

The bullfrog surfaced and clambered onto a damp rock to regard the children with keen, glistening eyes.

Fable laughed. "Don't worry. Kallra isn't mean—even though she never plays with me, not even when she's being a girl. Whenever I try to go swimming with her, she turns back into a frog and hides, but I think she's just shy. She shares her spring, though, so that's nice of her. Hi, Kallra!" Fable waved at the bullfrog, who croaked politely.

"So Kallra is some sort of a nymph?"

"Kinda. Mama calls her a nature spirit. There's lots of different nature spirits in the Wild Wood."

Cole stared at the frog. "Um. Hello," he said.

The bullfrog's eyes shone brightly. She studied Cole for a few more seconds, and then dove back into the clear water. For just a moment, beyond the reflected image of the treetops bouncing in the ripples, Cole saw a pretty, blue-green face peering up at him intensely from underwater. The figure spun, and then the girl was gone.

"I think she likes you," said Fable. "Ooh—watch the reflections!"

"The reflections?" said Cole.

"That's Kallra's special thing," Fable explained. "If she wants to, she can show you hints about your future in the reflections in her pool."

They stared at the pond's surface as the ripples gradually faded. Cole could see the sky above them, the bright canopy of green leaves, and the dark outlines of the tree trunks. He leaned over the edge for a better look. His own face peered back at him. He glanced toward Fable. She was uncharacteristically focused, her brow crinkled and her lips tight as she watched the surface. Cole turned back to the pool.

His own face in the water had changed. He blinked. The face staring back at him still looked like his—it had the same nose, the same eyes—but it had become somehow harder, older. Cole squinted and leaned his head this way and that. Maybe it was just the soil beneath the surface, but he could have sworn that the shadow of a beard now colored his chin. The man in Cole's reflection—it was definitely a man now and not a boy—had heavy bags beneath his eyes and wore a ragged gray cloak that Cole had never seen before. Cole raised a hand to touch his cheek, and the man's hand rose to his own. The man wore a simple silver band on his ring finger. A tingle scurried up Cole's spine. His chest felt tight.

"D-Dad?" he breathed.

Without warning, the earth shook.

The pond's surface rippled into a million fractured images of Cole, his eyes wide and his mouth hanging open. He fell back onto the grass, his head reeling, as if waking abruptly from a dream. "Wh-what's going on?"

"Earthquake," Fable said. "They keep happening lately. I don't know why. It'll be over soon, though. There we go."

The tremor eased and stopped. Cole turned back to the pond, but its surface was a mosaic of repeating forests in miniature.

"Did you see him?" Cole asked.

"Him?" said Fable.

Cole bit his lower lip and leaned over the water while the surface slowly cleared again. The scores of images melted into dozens, and then gradually into one. Cole stared at his reflection, holding his breath. Nothing happened. There was no world-weary man staring back at him, just a dusty boy.

"I think it's over," said Fable. "Kallra only ever gives you a tiny peek. She actually talks to my mama, sometimes. It's not fair. What did you see?"

Cole didn't answer right away. He was still peering into the water. A flicker of movement caught his eye, and he found himself looking past his own face into the darkness below it. On the muddy bottom of the pool, two glimmering green eyes stared up at him. The bullfrog spun and vanished into a muddy cloud. Where it had been, a perfectly round rock was visible for just a moment before the silt settled on top of it.

"Come on," said Fable. "I'll show you some other stuff."

"Wait a second," said Cole. He rolled up his sleeve and reached into the pool. His fingers brushed the loose mud, finding nothing at first, so he leaned in farther. The cold water soaked through his shirt and chilled his chest and shoulders until his hand finally closed around a hard, smooth disc. He pulled it up, shaking the wet dirt and droplets from it.

Fable peered over Cole's shoulder as he turned the rock around in his hand. It fit easily in his palm, only a little wider and thicker than a silver dollar. It had a hole at one end, as though perhaps it had once been hung from a string. Its surface was carved with an intricate design.

"Is that a tree?" said Cole.

"Maybe," said Fable. "Lucky. Kallra never gives me anything."

"What does it mean?"

Fable shrugged.

"Do you think I can keep it?" said Cole. "Would that be okay?"

"Duh," said Fable. "A lady in a lake just gave you a present. It'd be rude not to. Didn't your mama ever teach you basic manners?"

"I don't think someone who pees behind a bush is allowed to lecture me about manners."

"I only peed behind the bush because you got all weird when I started to pee in *front* of the bush. Jeesh. Everybody pees, Cole. It's not like I peed on a pixie ring. I'm not about to make that mistake twice. Hey, you wanna see a pixie ring?"

Cole turned the disc over and over in his hand as Fable led him onward through the Wild Wood. His feet stumbled, but his mind was racing. If the nature spirit had really wanted him to have this, then it had to be related to his vision, right? Did this mean his father was definitely still out there? Would the stone somehow help them find him? This could be the first clue in thirteen years that might connect Cole to his own long-lost family.

"What the snot happened here!"

Cole looked up to follow Fable's horrified gaze.

All around them, the ferns and grasses had been trampled down, and several limbs had been lopped off the trees nearby. A little way ahead, the tree trunks thinned out and rolling grassy hills began.

"Looks like somebody else came exploring through here first," said Cole. "Where are we?"

"Not a place that people are supposed to go exploring! This part of the forest is extra special. There's a sacred Grandmother Tree right over—" Fable stopped. "Wait. It should be right up ahead. We should be able to see it from here."

"Maybe you got turned around," suggested Cole. "Let's—whoa!"

Cole pitched forward abruptly, slamming hard onto the forest floor, one leg jammed deep into a hole in the earth.

"Ow!" he managed.

"And what is THAT?" Fable demanded.

Cole pulled himself out of the hole. His hip was sore from the landing, but miraculously he did not appear to have turned an ankle or broken anything. The hole into which he had stumbled was perfectly circular and only a bit wider than a dinner plate. It went straight down, deeper than he could see. His foot had not felt a bottom. "You know any giant gophers?" he said.

"This was not gophers." Fable narrowed her eyes. She reached a hand up to feel the fresh sap dripping from the severed tree branch. "Mama is not going to be happy about this."

The stone Cole had gotten from Kallra had been knocked out of his grasp by the fall, but it had only bounced a few feet away and come to rest in a pile of pine needles. Cole bent down to retrieve it, but as he rose, he felt a crawling, prickling sensation on the back of his hand. He swiped at his wrist instinctively, and connected with something that felt decidedly heavier than an insect. It gave a screechy squawk as it flew through the air, and then landed with a plop next to the hole.

"Sorry!" Cole stepped toward it and stood over the crumpled creature. It was a miniature person, no more than five or six inches tall, built like a sturdy tree branch. Its legs and arms looked as though they had been woven out of flexible twigs. Cole could not tell if the figure was wearing tiny wooden armor or if it simply had a chest that resembled tree bark. One of its sticklike legs was bent and badly splintered. It breathed heavily as it attempted to right itself.

"Oh, jeez. Sorry, little guy," said Cole. "Or girl? Woodperson? I didn't mean to—um. You were just on my hand, and I . . . Sorry."

The creature turned, its face a tiny mask of indignant rage.

"Are you a nature spirit? Hey, Fable! Come over here. I found a—a thing. What is this?"

Fable tromped back over the flattened foliage. "What did you—" She froze. "Oh crud."

"What? What is it?"

"Spriggan."

"The ones with the tempers and the grudges?" Cole whispered.

"Whatever you do," Fable said soberly, "do *not* make it mad."

"You mean, like, maybe don't slap it across the forest?" Cole whispered back.

110

"Why would you even think that? Are you crazy? Definitely don't do that!"

Cole swallowed hard.

The spriggan chittered like a furious squirrel, not taking its beady eyes off the boy.

"What do you mean?" Fable barked indignantly. "*This* mess? Absolutely not! We didn't have anything to do with this. We just got here."

The spriggan chirped angrily again, and then straightened and pulled a loose stick out of its back. The stick emerged with a faint *shhing*, like a knife being drawn from a sheath. Its end was polished ivory and looked very, very sharp.

"Hold on," Fable said. "Cole didn't do anything wrong. He's allowed to be here. He's my guest. Just wait a minute . . ."

"Easy, little guy," Cole said. He held out his hands peaceably. "We're not gonna hurt you."

The creature seemed to let down its guard for a moment, but then its expression faltered. It stared at the disc still cupped in Cole's palm, and then its sinewy muscles tensed and it shrieked, redoubling its fury. It shifted its footing, leaning its weight on its one good leg as if preparing to leap, and raised the ivory blade over its head.

Fable dove through the air, and with a muffled *fwumph*, she landed between Cole and the spriggan—not as a girl

111

but as an adolescent bear, her teeth bared and her hackles up. She growled fiercely. In the moment's hesitation that her sudden appearance gave the creature, Fable batted it hard with a swipe of her paw.

The spriggan stumbled backward, teetering on the edge of the deep hole. Cole stared at it unblinking. The creature swayed on the brink.

In a blur, Fable was a girl again. "Now would be a really great time for this to work," she murmured to herself. She took a deep breath—and then she concentrated. The leaves all around them began to dance along the flattened ground as the breeze picked up. Fable felt a twinge of pride. It wasn't exactly a *gale*, but it was working.

The spriggan very nearly steadied itself as it braced against the breeze, but then its bad leg gave out with an audible snap, and it fell backward into the darkness of the hole. Its furious cry lasted for several long seconds before it was cut short by a faint thump.

"I guess it isn't bottomless," whispered Cole.

"Oh crud, oh crud, oh crud," said Fable. She lifted her eyes slowly from the pit to Cole. "So," she said, "we should run."

TWELVE

"An' that, lad, is how Gripp ap Mull used a crafty bargain, a turkey carcass, and an old boot ta wipe Brigalia off the map forever." Kull tapped the incomprehensible chart behind him proudly.

"I've never even heard of Brigalia," said Tinn, rubbing his eyes. "Where is that?"

"Otch! It *isn't*! Were ya na paying attention ta a word of the story?"

"Sorry. It was a long story. I liked the part about the monkey."

"Aye. Of course ya did. That's the best bit." Kull hummed as he rolled up the scrolls littering the cave floor.

"Goblish history is interesting and everything," said Tinn. "And I had fun practicing my howls last night . . ."

"Yer makin' fine progress there."

". . . but I was wondering if maybe we could work on transformations again."

"Again? We were at it fer hours yesterday."

"I know—it's just . . . I want to be able to control it."

Kull tossed up his hands. "Otch. Far too much time as a human." He shook his head. "Goblins dinna *control* magic. That's na the point o' any of this. We give it a nudge now an' again, an' we let it do what it needs ta do. The universe knows what shape it wants ta be."

"But I need to," said Tinn.

"Hm." Kull stalked over to the mouth of the cave and peered down at the choppy waters far below them. "Ya know how ta swim?"

"I don't need swimming lessons, Kull, I need magic lessons."

"I asked if ya know how ta swim."

Tinn rolled his eyes. "Yes. I know how to swim. I learned when I was a little kid. We go swimming in a pond out by the quarry sometimes."

"Then hop in."

Tinn paused. "What?"

"Ya know how ta do it in a pond, so in ya pop. Go fer a swim."

Tinn stepped up to the opening and peered down as the waves crashed against the rocks.

"I'm not jumping in there. That water is crazy."

"Hm. Thought ya knew how," said Kull. "Water's water, na? Just make the water act like yer wee pond back home."

"I know how to swim, not how to control the waters I'm swimming in."

Kull smiled. He waggled his bristly eyebrows.

"Oh," said Tinn. "Wait. Is that a metaphor?"

"Is it?" Kull sauntered back to hop up on his battered stool.

Tinn's brow furrowed. "Okay. So, learning magic is like . . . learning how to swim," he said. "And instead of controlling the magic—I'm just sort of letting it carry me. And all this practice is just teaching myself how to let it carry me in the way I want to go. Is that about it?"

Kull nodded. "Universe tends ta give us what we need when we need it. It's our job ta catch the drift."

Tinn nodded and then turned back to watch the waves for another minute. A motion to his right caught his attention and he leaned out. A short, skinny goblin in a leather skullcap was hurrying toward their cave along the rickety gangplank that hung from the face of the cliff. Several of the lower platforms had burst into life as well, goblins of all shapes and sizes erupting into a flurry of activity.

"Come on, then," Kull said, sliding off his stool. "Let's work on yer Goblish alphabet fer a bit, an' then give transformation a try again after lunch."

"I think something's happening," said Tinn.

Kull crossed the cave to Tinn's side just as the skinny goblin sprang into view in front of them, panting.

"Kid's gotta go," she huffed. "Nudd's orders."

Kull and Tinn exchanged glances.

Chief Nudd was shouting commands at his lieutenants when Tinn and Kull reached the diplomatic chambers. A pair of stout goblins were jabbering as they hauled a broad oak table from one end of the cave to the other, catching its corners on every piece of furniture in the crowded room as they tried to rotate it. Half a dozen other goblins were zipping around them in a sort of busy panic that suggested that they probably had no idea what they were doing, but were not going to be caught sitting idly by not doing it. A scrawny whelp with knobby legs pushed past Tinn carrying a tray of glasses and bottles, and nearly lost the lot of them as he stumbled into the cave.

"Otch, ya drewgi!" Nudd barked at him. "Na the rum! Ya tryin' ta cause a bloody incident wi' that swill? Fetch the—the—oh, what's it called? The red one—in the fancy bottle."

"The one we use fer strippin' rust?"

"Aye. That one. An bring the nice cups."

The chief caught sight of Tinn and Kull for the first time. "Is he still here?"

"Of course he's still here," said Kull. "Got hours o' lessons planned fer him yet."

"My mom's not gonna be back to pick me up until late," said Tinn.

"Change o' plans, I'm afraid. Kull here will have ta walk ya back home a bit early."

"Am I in trouble?" said Tinn.

"Na. Touch o' politics, is all. Unexpected meeting cropped up. An envoy of spriggans is due shortly, and the spriggan stance on human relations is—erm—rather old-fashioned."

"Tinn is as much a goblin as the rest o' us," Kull bristled. "Should hear his howls. Right proud, I am."

Nudd patted Tinn on the shoulder. "I'm sure yer comin' along just fine, lad. Thing is, yer still, well . . ." He gestured to Tinn's face.

"He made hisself green an' spotty fer a full ten minutes yesterday," said Kull. "We were gonna work on the ears an' teeth after lunch."

117

"Please, sir," said Tinn. "I'll stay inside with Kull the whole time they're here."

"I told yer mum I'd keep ya safe," said Nudd. "Around spriggans is the opposite o' safe, especially fer a human. An' refusing a formal envoy from the colony is the opposite o' safe fer the horde. Afraid my decision is final. There'll be other days, lad. Give him yer lesson on the road this time, Kull. Oi! I said no flowers!" Nudd directed this last outburst at one of his scurrying subordinates. "Think our guests wanna see a bunch o' dying plants stuffed in a pot?" The chief went back to preparations, and Kull led Tinn out of the cave and up the narrow ledge into the Wild Wood.

"Which ones are spriggans?" said Tinn as they picked their way along the goblin path. "They're a sort of fairy, right?"

"Fairies often claim them, aye," said Kull. "But they're na really fair folk. The forest wouldn't abide 'em iffin they were. They're spirits by right. Force o' nature. Vindictive things. They've na forgiven humans."

"Forgiven us? What have humans done?"

Kull raised an eyebrow. "Take a lot longer than we've got ta put that list together, lad. Humans an' magic folk got a long an' nasty history. People used to kill magical creatures fer sport, ya know, or else catch 'em and force 'em ta serve humankind. Stuffed genies inta bottles, pressed pixies inside books, hunted dragons near ta extinction. Don't need ta go inta the details. Rough stuff. Right wicked."

"That's awful," said Tinn.

"That's what the spriggans thought. Made themselves unofficial guardians o' the wild long ago. They protect the oddlings and the forest from humankind, protect the boundaries, that sorta thing. Right ornery buggers. No sense o' humor at all."

"What do they look like?"

"Wee, ugly things, most o' the time," said Kull. "They've got skin like slivered rocks and tree bark. Easy ta miss out here in the wood. When they get angry, though—something else comes out o' them. There are those that say spriggans are the spirits o' the giants that used to live in this world a long time ago, and they become giants again when the rage takes them."

They walked in silence while Tinn considered this.

"Were there really giants?" he said at last. "There are lots of stories about them, but they all sound unbelievable, living up in the clouds and saying things like 'fee-fi-fo-fum' and 'I'll grind his bones to make my bread' and stuff like that."

Kull made a noise that might have been a laugh. "Otch. Stories like that are half the reason spriggans still don't like your lot. Of course there was giants. They's long since died off now, but they used to live all over the place. The clouds bit is silly—giants never lived on clouds—and the 'fee-fi-fo-fum' is downright insultin'. How would you like it if I mocked yer language like that? As fer the grindin' bones—well, that's more what you'd call a cultural misunderstandin'."

"Giants *didn't* threaten to grind up people's bones?"

"Well. They said it, sure, but it was ne'er a threat."

"How is that *not* a threat?"

"Otch. Context. Different rites an' traditions fer different groups. Lotta cultures value ritual cannibalism as a sorta tribute, ya see? They say consumin' remains can fill ya with the spirit of the deceased. It was a way of honoring the dead in the past by letting them live within you. 'I'll grind yer bones ta make my bread' is a pretty fair translation, aye, but fer the giants it was a friendly expression. Like 'Hey, mate. I think yer grand. When ya die I'll eat yer bits so ya live on forever.' That kinda thing."

"That's super gross," said Tinn, "but I think I understand."

"What do humans do ta honor their dead?" asked Kull.

"We bury them," said Tinn.

"In the dirt?" said Kull. "Like ya bury a poo? Hardly see how that's a respectful way ta treat yer kin."

"Well, there's a whole ceremony and a coffin."

"What's a coffin?"

"It's a fancy box for dead people."

"Ah," said Kull. "I suppose it's probably nice."

"What do goblins do with your dead?"

"We use 'em, mostly. Fuel fer the engines. Bones are great fer makin' tools. Nice ta think I'll be useful when I'm gone. Hate ta go ta waste in some box. Being bread sounds nice, though, too. I could enjoy bein' a warm baguette."

"I guess," said Tinn. He trod in silence for several paces.

"How about you?" Kull asked. "What would you wanna be?"

"Not dead?" said Tinn.

Kull chuckled. "Grand job so far. Let's see if we can keep it up just a wee bit longer, eh?"

Before Tinn could reply, the ground trembled beneath their feet. Birds in the trees around them took flight in a burst of tweets and screeches.

"Just another quake," said Kull. "Happenin' a lot lately."

Nonetheless, they quickened their pace as they made their way out of the woods. Kull said his goodbyes at the edge of the forest, and Tinn walked the rest of the way home by himself.

"Cole?" Tinn yelled from the back porch when he reached the house. A tingle rippled up his neck. It was strange, really, how much easier it was to be alone in a place where you expected to be alone than it was to be alone in a place where you expected people to greet you. He kicked a pebble off the back step.

His mother was supposed to be at work, Tinn remembered—the new job. Cole was probably with her, tucked away behind the dry goods or getting into trouble for pocketing sweets. Tinn would meet them there. He latched the door and hurried off down the road toward town.

THIRTEEN

"YOU'RE NOT DEAD!" SAID FABLE. "THAT'S A GOOD way to end an adventure, right?"

Cole nodded, panting. He was on the edge of town now, the forest behind him. Fable hung back at the tree line, grinning widely. They had emerged from the forest at the north end of the village, out near the old mill, but Cole could find his way from here without any trouble.

"You sure you don't wanna come hang out with me in town for a little while?" said Cole.

"Can't," said Fable. "My mama says it's too dangerous."

"Sure." Cole might have laughed if he was not still out of breath from racing through the forest with the sounds of crunching leaves and snapping branches behind him. "Yeah. Indoor plumbing and bakeries are scary stuff. Not like that peaceful forest full of homicidal monsters."

"Plumbing *does* sound exciting," said Fable. "You should show me some if my mama ever lets me visit again."

Cole bid her goodbye, and Fable waved before hopping back over the fallen tree. "Hey, Fable," Cole called after her. "I had a fun time with you. I think you'd be a great Witch of the Wood."

"Run away with me again sometime?"

"Definitely."

Cole found himself smiling as he kicked his way down the dusty road. The sun was already high in the sky. It still felt strange, having had a whole day—and a whole adventure—without Tinn. In a few hours, they would make their way back through the forest to pick him up again, and Cole would listen as Tinn told him all the exciting things he had done, but this time Cole would have something just as exciting to share in return.

A harried shout echoed down the road, and Cole stopped. He turned around. The road behind him led north, toward nothing but old farmlands and the abandoned mill. People almost never came out this way.

"Help!" the voice called.

Cole's eyes widened. He followed the sound of the cries cautiously up the empty street until he rounded a bend and found two men shuffling toward him, their clothes covered head to toe in dust, one of them leaning heavily on the other's shoulders.

"You! Boy, lend a hand!" yelled the first man. It took a moment for Cole to place him under the layers of dirt.

"Mr. Hill?" said Cole. "What happened?"

"We were attacked!" said Jacob Hill. "Take his other arm."

The other man looked up and Cole realized with a start that it was Evie's father. His eyes were wild and his hair was tousled and trickled grit and dust with every motion.

"Mr. Warner? Oh, jeez. It's gonna be all right. It's me, Cole. I'm a friend of your daughter's, remember? Here, you can lean on me."

"G-g-giant," stammered Oliver Warner.

"A giant?" said Cole. "What are you talking about?"

Warner's face was pale, and he was limping heavily. He grimaced and swayed for a moment as he shifted some of his weight to Cole's shoulder. "Giant," he breathed again.

"You must have seen it looming over the treetops!" Hill cut in. "It was three stories tall if it was an inch!"

"An actual giant?" said Cole. "Where?" He craned his neck to look backward, and Warner groaned.

"Vanished," said Hill. "Back into the forest somewhere. Barely got out with our lives. Warner here was working on the drill frame when it appeared. I glanced down at my schematics, and when I looked up it was right there, big as anything. The thing came out of nowhere. Four stories tall. Maybe five. Lambert and Stokes ran for the hills. Can't blame them. I expect they're halfway to Glanville by now. Warner only just jumped free from the scaffolds before the brute could crush him, and then it thundered off into the woods."

"Whoa," said Cole.

"And here I thought Warner's uncle was just a superstitious old man," Hill mused. "That forest really is trying to kill us."

Cole glanced back into the woods again. Somewhere in there, a massive monster lurked. He wished that Fable had decided to come with him after all. Sure, she had been able to take on a miniature twig-man with a swat of her paw—but up against a creature five stories tall, it was Fable who would look like a twig.

Tinn made his way alone up Endsborough's main street. The sun felt warm on his cheeks, and he could smell meat and onions frying in the kitchen of the Lucky Pig. It must be nearly lunchtime already. He wondered if his mother would let him and Cole have a little something from the shop. He waved hello to Old Mrs. Stewart in the rocking chair on her porch. Behind her stood stout barrels of freshly husked hazelnuts, waiting to be carted off to the big city. He smiled at Mr. Washington delivering the mail, then he passed the empty schoolhouse as he cut across the town square to the general store. The bell chimed as he opened the door.

"Tinn?" His mother looked down at him over a counter full of hair treatments and shaving accessories. She was the only person who never hesitated to tell the two of them apart. "What on earth—?"

"Hi, Mom!" said Tinn. "There was a whole thing at the cliff. It's okay, though. I'm fine. Kull brought me home. Where's Cole?" Tinn fiddled with a swiveling mirror next to the tins of shaving powder. His face popped into view magnified, his nose several sizes too big.

"Stop touching things. Cole's back at the house."

"No, he's not."

Annie pursed her lips. *Of course he isn't.* "He's back in *trouble*, then. Best you're not in it with him, for once. I'm glad you're safe and sound. Mr. Zervos is sending me for my lunch break in about twenty minutes. Do you think you can wait out front until then?"

Tinn nodded. He eyed the beef jerky on the counter hopefully.

Annie shook her head. "You have perfectly good food waiting for you at home," she said.

"What's this?" Mr. Zervos called behind Annie. He emerged from the ice cellar and closed the door behind him with a click. Mr. Zervos was a friendly man with a big peppery mustache and a bushy beard. According to Mrs. Stewart, who was older than almost anybody in town, Mr. Zervos had once had the sort of figure people called *barrel-chested*, like the strong men in the fitness magazines he sold at the front of the shop. If that was the case, then the barrel had slipped down into his stomach years ago, and was now supported only by the stalwart efforts of a heroic belt.

"Ah, the boys!" He beamed.

"Just the one this time," said Annie.

"Tinn," said Tinn.

"I thought the two of you were a package deal. Ah, well. Come to see your mother work, young man? She'll be running this shop in no time!"

"You're very kind, Mr. Zervos. I'm still just happy to have work. Tinn is going to wait out front for me to take my lunch. He won't be a bother."

No sooner had she said it than Tinn's sleeve caught

the swiveling mirror and it slapped glass-down against the countertop with a sharp *crack*.

"*Ooch!*" Mr. Zervos winced.

"I'm sorry!" Tinn righted the mirror. "It didn't break. It's okay!" A small stack of pomade tins toppled over as his elbow swung wide. They rolled onto the floor with a series of bangs. "Shoot! I'm so sorry! I'll get them!"

Annie caught a teetering jar of lather and righted it. "I told you not to touch anything."

"I'm so sorry. I'm always screwing stuff up." He deposited an armful of pomade tins back on the counter. A glimmer caught his eye and he bent down to retrieve a discarded penny, too. "Here," he added, holding out a coin to Mr. Zervos.

"Ah, ah, ah." Mr. Zervos shook his head. He was smiling beneath his bushy beard. "None of that. Breaking a mirror is very bad luck, yes. But you did *not*! So that is lucky! And finding a penny is good luck, too. Double lucky. You keep that. Don't fret so much about the bad luck that you forget to see the good. Eh?"

Tinn allowed himself a smile, but his ears still felt hot with embarrassment. He tucked the penny into his pocket.

"I'm all done with inventory," Mr. Zervos said. "Why don't you go ahead and take your lunch, Annie. Ah—but wait." He plucked two strips of jerky from the jar on the counter and slipped them to Tinn with a wink. "One for that brother of yours. Stay good for your mom, now."

"Yes, sir."

"Oh," said Annie. "That's terribly nice of you, sir. Are you sure? I can stay."

"I have managed on my own before, believe it or not. This town has seen more buildings explode in the past month than it's seen rushes on flour or baked beans. I'll be fine for an hour."

"Thank you very much."

Annie slipped off her apron and hung it neatly on a hook by the door to the back room. She and Tinn stepped out into the sunlight together.

"Sounds like work's going well," said Tinn. He munched on a strip of jerky and avoided making eye contact.

"Yes, other than your fidgeting fingers, I've had no problems so far," said Annie. She rapped a knuckle on the siding as she passed. "Knock on wood. What about you? How was the overnight? Did you get scared?"

"Naw. It was fine," said Tinn. "I'm learning a lot, and I'm starting to understand the changes a little more. We did songs this time, too. Well, Kull called them songs. There are lots of noises involved. I practiced my howl."

"We're howling now?" Annie said. "Okay. You didn't

have to hang off the side of a cliff for howls. If I had known you wanted to howl, we could be howling at home."

"Mom." Tinn rolled his eyes.

"We can howl right now, if you like."

"Stop, Mom. It's special howls. Never mind."

"I'm only teasing. I'm glad you had a nice time. I'll have to thank Mr. Kull for bringing you all the way back. Now if only I knew where your brother ran off to—"

Shouts rang out behind them. Mrs. Stewart stood up from her rocking chair to see what was the matter. A pair of stable hands nearby dropped the bags of feed they were carrying and jogged up to a commotion stirring in the town square.

"What in heaven's name is going on?" Annie held Tinn's hand tightly as they both turned toward the hubbub. "Is that . . . is that *Cole*?"

Three haggard figures staggered to a stop in the center of town. Cole and Mr. Hill carefully eased Oliver Warner— now as white as a sheet—down onto a bench. Hill didn't look much better. He collapsed at the foot of the bench, running his hands through his dusty hair. Amos Washington from the post office ran to summon Dr. Fisher and Old Jim.

Annie and Tinn pushed through the gawkers. "Cole! Are you all right? What happened? Where have you been?"

"I'm fine, Mom," Cole said through his mother's sleeve as she pulled him into a hug. "I wasn't even there."

"Tell us what happened, Hill!" a voice from the crowd barked. The square grew silent as all ears leaned in to listen.

Jacob Hill lifted his face from his hands. He considered for a moment before speaking. "The thing was six stories tall," he said at last. "A giant, ladies and gentlemen! It was on us in an instant. Smashed the drill site to pieces. The rest of the crew took off running, but I went back for Mr. Warner. I owed him that much."

A murmur rippled through the crowd.

"What was it?" called Helen Grouse, from the back of the group.

"It was an unnatural thing, my friends." Hill took a deep breath. "There and not there, all at once! It made my eyes ache just to look at it, but it was solid enough. I can still hear the sound of the metal twisting under its grip, bending like it was taffy. It was a brute to put Goliath to shame, a veritable mountain of muscles and rage, an unbelievable sight to behold."

"There's no such thing as giants," somebody yelled. "He's lying!"

"It's all t-t-true," spluttered Oliver Warner, propping himself unsteadily on an elbow. "It was a giant. A real giant. I saw it with my own eyes. Hill saved me. He pulled the

132

planks off of me and dragged me out of there. Oh, Lord. Uncle Jim was right. It's all true. It's all true. It's all—" The exertion of speaking washed over him and Warner collapsed onto the bench. Around him, the crowd was filled with gasps as neighbors exchanged furtive looks.

Dr. Fisher arrived and made her way to the front of the crowd. The onlookers mumbled and whispered, and Oliver Warner moaned unintelligibly as the doctor examined him. She snipped the man's trousers up past the knee and gently shifted his leg. Mr. Warner groaned, his head rolling against the bench.

"It's definitely broken," Fisher announced. "I can give him something for the pain, but we'll want to get him cleaned up and into a proper bed before I set the bone."

A canvas litter was procured, and Mr. Warner was already being carried away when Evie and Old Jim came hurrying down the road.

"Dad?" Evie called. "Dad!"

Mr. Warner put out a hand limply to pat his daughter on the shoulder as she ran up to the cot. "I'll be okay, sweetie. Stay with . . . Uncle . . ." His voice petered out and the doctor pressed Evie out of the way.

Tinn stepped out from behind his mother and Cole and edged closer to Mr. Hill. "Was it really a giant?" he asked. "Are you sure?"

Hill shook his head. "Sure? Kid, this morning I was *sure* fairy tales were a bunch of cockamamie nonsense and that the worst thing in that forest was wolves. I'm not sure of anything anymore. I know what I saw, though."

Old Jim pursed his lips and nodded. "Was only a matter of time," he grunted. "Been warnin' folk about the Wild Wood fer years. There's evil in that forest."

"It's not *evil*," Tinn began, but a voice from the crowd cut him off.

"My cousin saw the witch once," yelled Albert Townshend, "out by the mines. He said he locked eyes on her for just a second, and the very next day he broke his leg."

"Our back acre's been cursed for years," called someone else from the back of the group. "My old man can never get anything but weeds to grow that close to the forest."

"I've still got a scar on my knee from a tussle with a hobgoblin that got into our attic years ago!"

"I *told* you to leave it alone, Stuart. They're not a bother unless they're provoked."

The crowd began to bubble various accounts of unnatural occurrences and brushes with beasts.

Hill was agog. "And this is just . . . just common knowledge? How do you all *live* like this?" he asked. "With evil forces lurking behind every log and leaf?"

"The forest folk are *not* evil!" Tinn said more loudly.

Old Jim raised an eyebrow. Cole stepped to Tinn's side.

"There *are* lots of dangerous things in there," said Evie timidly from beside her great uncle. "But maybe *evil* isn't the right word for—"

"No. *Evil* is right," growled Mr. Fenerty, a crotchety old man who ran the stationery shop. "Witches and ogres and . . . *goblins*." He let his eyes flick from one Burton boy to the other. "Creatures like that don't have an ounce of good in them."

There were murmurs of agreement from the crowd.

The air in the crowded town center felt suddenly thin. Tinn flinched as a hand gripped his shoulder, but when he looked up it was only his mother. "Ignore them," she whispered, but Tinn's pulse was pounding in his ears.

"You don't know," he blurted. "None of you knows! All you know are stories. Stories get things wrong."

"Stories didn't break my nephew's leg." Old Jim's voice was cold.

"Tinn's right, Jim," said Annie. "We don't know what really happened up there."

"I know what I saw," Hill grumbled.

"Mm." Old Jim scowled. "Show 'em."

"What?" said Hill.

"Show 'em what happened to yer rig. They don't wanna listen to my *stories*. So let 'em see for themselves."

Hill looked less than eager at the prospect of returning to the scene, but with an audience awaiting his response, he nodded resolutely. "Yes. Yes, of course. I'll take you. You, and anyone else brave enough to witness the wreckage with their own eyes."

The crowd erupted into a susurrus as curious townsfolk stepped up to join the expedition. Annie knelt down in front of the boys.

"The forest *isn't* evil," mumbled Tinn. "*I'm* not evil."

"Of course you're not, sweetie." Annie kissed his forehead. "You know better than to take those knuckleheads seriously. Old Jim thinks electricity is evil."

Tinn nodded glumly.

"The rest of the town seems to be taking him pretty seriously," said Cole.

"Yes. I think it might be best if I go up there with them," Annie whispered. "I don't love the idea of giants in Endsborough, but I don't love the thought of a bunch of frightened townspeople egging each other on to go hunting monsters, either. Somebody needs to keep a level head."

"Let's go," said Cole. "We should tell Fable and her mom what we find. They keep tabs on everything that happens in their woods—they're not gonna like this."

"*I* will tell them what *I* find," Annie corrected. "I don't want you two anywhere near that place."

"What?" said both boys at once.

"But, Mom—" Cole began.

"No buts. I want you to stick together, go straight back home, and wait for me there. Understood?"

"No way. If anybody knows what to look for out there, it's us," argued Tinn. "We know more about things in those woods than anyone else in town."

"Yes. And they've almost been the death of you more times than I care to count. I mean it." Annie stood up. Twenty or so villagers were already beginning to make their way up the road behind her. "Go home. Stay put."

"Yes, ma'am," they said in miserable unison.

Annie took a deep breath and hurried after the crowd.

Tinn and Cole watched their mother join the procession. They kept watching until the group had made its way out of sight beyond the first bend.

Tinn looked at Cole. Cole looked at Tinn.

They did not go home, and they did not stay put.

FOURTEEN

TINN AND COLE DID NOT IMMEDIATELY FOLLOW the adults up the dusty street to the Roberson Hills. The forest and the town nestled into each other like puzzle pieces along that road, the route weaving in and out, following a path older than Endsborough itself. It was an old loggers' road that dated back to the days when the town had been little more than an outpost and the mill had still been under construction.

"I have an idea," said Tinn. "But I'm pretty sure it's a bad one."

"Sounds about right," said Cole. "Bad ideas are kind of

what we do. Usually *my* bad ideas, though, so I guess it's your turn. What are you thinking?"

"I think we'll get there faster if we cut through the forest," said Tinn. "The Roberson Hills are pretty much straight north. The road goes way over to the west and then circles back, so if we cut straight up while they follow the road, then we can get there *before* everybody else."

"I'm in," said Cole. He took a deep breath. "Let's go into the Wild Wood. Eyes out for giants. And no getting captured by shadows or anything this time. Ready?"

"Ready."

"Ready," said a third voice, slightly breathlessly, from behind them.

Cole and Tinn turned.

Evie was wearing a sturdy plaid dress, a pair of over-sized work boots, and an eager expression. A set of plain brown journals bounced at her hip on a book strap.

"Oh. I don't know if—" Tinn began.

"I'm coming with you," said Evie. "Something out there attacked my dad, and I'm going to see what it was for myself. I've been training for this forever."

"You've been training for . . . giants?" said Cole.

"I've got a whole section on giants." Evie patted her journals.

Cole and Tinn exchanged glances.

"Don't leave me out. My dad told me to stay with Uncle Jim, and then Uncle Jim told me to go stay with my dad, and so for the first time ever, nobody is here to tell me I can't. I might not get another chance like this one. Please."

"We're kinda in a hurry," said Cole.

"Great, then we'd better get going." Evie held tight to her book strap with both hands and marched between them into the forest.

The thing about roads—even winding ones—is that they are designed for traveling. The thing about forests is that they are not. Twenty minutes later, the children were still making their way through the merciless Wild Wood. Twice they reached an impasse and had to double back to find another way around.

"Exploring the unexplored forest," Cole grunted, "was a lot easier when we had a map and there was a trail."

"Are you doing okay?" Tinn asked, helping pull Evie over a rock nearly as tall as she was. "We can stop for a rest if you need."

"I'm fine," Evie said, but Tinn could see her wince as her feet landed on the forest floor.

"I'm pretty sure we should have gotten there by now," said Cole. He peered into the forest ahead. It showed no signs of thinning. "This bad idea of yours might have actually been a bad idea."

"Are we lost?" said Evie.

"No," said Tinn. "We're not lost."

"We might be a little bit lost," admitted Cole.

"Well, of course we're a *little bit* lost," said Tinn. "We're on an adventure."

A bird screeched from somewhere nearby, and the branches beside them shook and then fell still. The forest grew quiet.

"Is there . . . is there something in that tree?" Evie whispered.

"No," said something in the tree.

Evie froze. Tinn froze. Cole froze.

The tree, being a tree, remained more or less frozen.

"Gotcha! It's me!" Fable stuck her head out from behind the trunk and laughed. She swung gracefully to a lower branch and then to the forest floor with a soft *thump*.

"Fable!" said Evie.

"Hi, friends! What are you all doing in the forest? Were you hiding? I totally found you."

"Something's happened," said Tinn. "There was an attack."

"Oh," Fable said. The smile fell from her face and she scowled. "The forest *has* been acting kinda hinky and rustly today. I wonder if it's been trying to tell me. Trees are super bad at saying stuff."

"My dad got attacked by a giant from the forest," said Evie. "The town is pretty worked up about it."

"A giant?" said Fable. "I *wish*. We don't have anything like that in the Wild Wood. Mama says there used to be all kinds of giant creatures in here—people giants, bird giants, funny-colored ox giants—but that was way before she was the queen. They're all gone now. There's moose, I guess. Moose are pretty big. Was it a moose?"

"No, not a moose," said Cole. "Mr. Hill said it was three stories tall—or maybe six. It got a little confusing. He described it like a huge, angry person."

"I don't think I've ever seen anything like that before. How tall is a story? That seems like a funny way to measure something. I've heard some really long ones, but some stories are pretty short, too."

"Not like that," said Cole. "A *story*, like buildings have stories."

"I bet buildings don't have as many stories as the forest has," said Fable.

"Fable, no," Cole said.

"*I* have stories," Evie cut in, "about giants in the forest. Hang on, maybe this could help." They turned toward her. She tugged one of the journals out of her book strap and riffled through the entries until she found what she was looking for. "How about this one?" She held out the page so that they could see. "They're called *kee-wakw*. They're supposed to be man-eating giants with icy hearts who roam the woods from here all the way up to Quebec."

"Where's Quebec?" said Tinn.

"I'm pretty sure that's not a real place," said Cole.

"Whoa!" Fable marveled, taking the book from Evie and flipping through the pages. "There's giants made out of rocks and ones made out of ice. And there's other stuff, too—here's a page about hinkypunks. Neat! I wonder how Candlebeard is doing. Ooh, there's pictures on some of these pages! This book is amazing!"

"Huh," said Tinn, peeking over Fable's shoulder. "This *is* pretty impressive."

"We don't know if any of that stuff is true, though," Cole said. "That's all just stories Old Jim told her."

"But it's written down," said Fable, "in books."

"They're just my journals," said Evie.

"What's *journals*?" said Fable.

"They're books that Evie wrote," explained Tinn.

"Oh my gosh—you can WRITE BOOKS?" Fable stared at Evie, eyes wide.

Evie nodded. "Well, sure. Anybody can."

"And you drew the pictures, too?" Fable said.

Evie nodded. "They're not perfect, but they're the best I could do without seeing it all for myself."

"Ooh! I've seen things for myself! Loads of things. Can I help you write books?"

"You . . . want to help me add to my journals?"

"Sure! I can show you the very best forest stuff." Fable nodded. "And then you can make it all book-shaped!"

"Are you kidding me? Yes! Yes—that sounds amazing!"

"We really should be going," Cole said.

"Do you have a page for wind blossoms?" Fable snatched a sprig of half a dozen peach-colored flowers from the base of a tree. Two bulbous pink petals curled away from the center of each bloom. "Their proper name is *Antipugeum*. Mama made me learn *lots* of plants."

"Pretty. They look like snapdragons," said Evie.

"Nope!" Fable giggled. "Watch this!" She gave the base of the flower a squeeze and the petals spread open with a whispered *prrppth*.

"I think Evie's right," said Tinn. "I'm pretty sure those are snap—oh Lord!" He slapped a hand over his nose. "What is that *smell*?"

Fable erupted into giggles as the other children staggered back from the putrid plant. "Farts! It's farts! They smell like farts. Their name means *counterfeit buttocks*. Aren't they great?" She squeezed the fetid flower so that its twin pink petals wiggled again. "Each one's only got one really good poot in it. Here, you can do the next ones!" Fable handed the remaining handful of blooms to Evie.

"Oh, um. Thanks," said Evie. "I think I'll . . . save mine, though." She tucked the blossoms very gingerly into the pocket of her dress.

"Hey," Cole cut in. "Maybe we can talk about books and farts and stuff when we're *not* trying to get somewhere in a hurry? The grown-ups will be there any minute now. Fable, do you know where the Roberson Hills are?" Cole asked.

"Nope," she answered. She returned the journal to Evie, who tightened it back into its strap. "Are they near Quebec?"

"No. They're near the edge of the forest," said Tinn. "It's a really lumpy area next to some farmland with an old swayback barn."

"I know that place!" Fable brightened. "It's not far— right up that next ridge and past a little thicket." Fable leapt into action, hopping over a rotten log and between a pair of mossy boulders. Cole was right behind her. Tinn followed closely at first, but he paused when he noticed Evie lagging. He waited at the top of the rise for her to catch up.

"I can do it," she huffed. "Thanks, though." Tinn hadn't thought about it before, but for every step the boys took, Evie had to take two. The forest must feel twice as vast to her.

"It's fine. Catch your breath for a second," said Tinn. Evie nodded and leaned against a sloping rock.

"Are you guys coming?" Cole called from up ahead. Tinn could hear the anxious energy in his brother's voice.

Evie pushed herself up, hiding a cringe of discomfort as she stood. "I can go faster," she said.

"We know which way to go now," said Tinn. He turned back to Cole. "We can meet you there," he called.

Cole hesitated. He looked at the forest ahead of them, then back at Tinn. "Are you sure?"

"Yeah. We're right behind you. We'll be fine."

They would not be fine. Perhaps, somewhere deep down, Cole suspected they would not be fine, but he gave Tinn a wary thumbs-up, anyway, and scrambled onward through the forest with Fable.

FIFTEEN

THE QUEEN OF THE DEEP DARK PACED ACROSS the empty glen. Fable was late.

It had not been a smooth morning. The entire forest seemed to be unraveling. The gnomes had brought her no less than three formal complaints about the brownies in as many hours, there were several reports of misconduct from wandering bogles, and a handful of nymphs had accused the hinkypunks of moving boundary markers overnight. The accused were all avoiding her and the accusers would not leave her alone. It was all the queen could do to remove herself from the throng of agitated forest folk in time for her daughter's lessons. And Fable was late.

A note of unquiet urgency echoed in the whipping wind. The queen turned her eyes to the canopy above her. The forest was tense. Something wasn't right.

Raina pursed her lips. Fable had been late to countless lessons, but she had never forgotten about one entirely. The more she considered it, the more she had to admit to herself that if there was trouble in the forest, Fable was probably already in the thick of it.

She pulled the cloak snug around her shoulders and turned her attention to the north. There, just on the edge of her senses, the forest was itching.

"Yer Majesty," came a voice from behind her before she could take the first step. Chief Nudd was stepping across the open grass to meet her. "A moment."

The queen narrowed her eyes to look at the goblin properly. Nudd had come with sentries, although they remained behind him, in the shadows of her forest. He stood just a little straighter than usual, and his hat had been recently buffed.

"This is an official visit, then?" she said.

"Afraid so," he said. "I've just had a meeting." He cleared his throat. "With the spriggans."

The queen kept her expression expertly blank. "I imagine you have many diplomatic encounters with factions of the Wild Wood. Business between forest folk and goblins is no concern of mine."

"It was about *you*," said Nudd. "Among other things."

"I see," she said. "Well. If spriggans wanted me to be privy to their dealings, I assume they would deal directly with me."

"Aye." Nudd took a deep breath. "I wager they will, soon enough."

"High Chief." The queen let the title rest in the air for a moment. "You cannot think that the spriggans, who spoke to you in confidence, won't know that you've come to me directly after your private meeting."

"I believe they are expectin' no less," said Nudd. "I imagine that's why my horde was the last faction they spoke to. They've already been ta all the dominant clans an' colonies o' the wood."

"Is that so?" The queen raised an eyebrow.

"Aye. The wild ones an' the spirits an' the oddlings. They're a thorough lot, spriggans are."

"And what did they want?"

"They want ta know if they can count on us ta be allies—or at least ta stay out of their way when the time comes."

"The time for what?"

"They were . . . unspecific as to the details. But they're carryin' their war satchels again. That's na good."

The queen remained silent for several seconds as she considered this. "So, the spriggans are preparing for a fight," she said.

"Looks that way," Nudd said. "They're right angry, Raina."

"The Grandmother Tree." The queen's voice was tight. The spriggans had always shown her respect. They had acknowledged her sovereignty over the Wild Wood for years. The only parts of the forest they did not recognize as her domain were the caves and tunnels that ran beneath the Deep Dark—which Raina had been more than happy to concede as sacred spriggan territory. Their purposes had always been aligned: the protection of the forest and the barriers between the human world and the wild. Why, now, would they defy her position?

The queen could feel an ingot of heat rising in her chest.

"They've always know that the queen began her life as a human. Raised by fair folk, but still human. They've never held that against ya. I think they understood ya ta be neutral—slighted by both sides, beholden to neither, loyal ta the forest alone. They are beginning to grow concerned, however"—Nudd took a deep breath—"that yer humanity is gettin' the better of ya, and with it yer born allegiance."

"That is ludicrous."

"Aye. That's what I told 'em." Nudd shrugged. "Said if they really thought the queen was goin' soft, they'd na be so afraid ta tell her ta her face. That got under the wee buggers' skin."

"How dare they question my loyalties? Do they not remember when I unleashed fury against the men who razed the forest in the west? I single-handedly revived the stories of the Witch of the Wood. Grown men whispered my titles. They refused to work, shut down their mill, and planted saplings to appease me, like an offering to the gods of old. The Queen of the Deep Dark is *legend*!" She took a slow, deep breath. "I have made myself no ally to human-kind. My only allegiance is to my mother's legacy and the duties she entrusted to me as a steward of this forest. My diligence has kept the Wild Wood safe as long as I have walked this earth."

"Aye," Nudd said gently. "You were a force ta be reck-oned with, Raina, and yer mother before ya. That's likely why they allowed ya free rein. But the saplings those men planted are twenty feet tall today. That was another age, lass, and they haven't seen the fury of the queen in some time. What they have seen are the marks of human hands on sacred lands, and the Witch of the Wood cavorting with townsfolk."

"I have never *cavorted* a day in my life," the queen said. "I will not apologize for protecting the lives of children."

Nudd held up his hands. "Ya dinna have ta tell me. I also reminded them that the forest has Tinn ta thank fer its renewed magic. But the spriggans still seem to have their doubts."

"Fine. They can question my neutrality all they like. But if they seek to contradict my authority or sow unrest in my forest, they may very well see the fury of the queen firsthand."

Nudd nodded approvingly. "Yer Majesty," he said, and turned to go.

"I wonder," the queen added. "What was your answer, Thief King?"

Nudd glanced back. "About what?"

"Will the goblins stand with the spriggans, when the time comes?" said the queen.

Nudd smirked. "That's one o' those funny things about goblins. We never seem ta know ourselves," he said, "until the time comes."

SIXTEEN

"THE QUEEN OF THE DEEP DARK," TINN READ aloud as he and Evie picked their way forward through the bracken. Evie had allowed him to flip through one of her journals as they traveled. "*Also known as the Witch of the Wild Wood. The story of the horrifying hag who haunts the forest begins with a love scorned.*" Tinn glanced up. "What's *scorned* mean?"

"They were going to get married, I think, but then he left her for someone else and broke her heart."

"Huh. What a jerk." Tinn felt like he should say more. "I wouldn't—" he began. "I mean. If I was in love . . . I would never . . . I mean—" He immediately wished he had said less. Reading was much easier than talking to Evie Warner.

"Huh?" said Evie.

Tinn turned his eyes hastily back to the page and continued. *"Soon to become a mother out of wedlock, the woman was shunned by her neighbors.* Man, everybody in this story is a jerk. *Destitute and alone, she learned to fend for herself, tending a humble garden and hunting or foraging in the forest on the edge of town. The woman had no one for company, save her daughter, whom she bore into the world alone in a drafty house on a stormy night. The child knew no suffering, though. It grew fat and healthy, with a laugh like tinkling bells. One day, the fairies heard the girl's sweet laughter and coveted the child. So they came and stole her away."* He turned the page. "This is a little different than the version I know," he said.

"It's the way Uncle Jim always tells it," said Evie. "Mostly. I left out the bad words."

Tinn read on. *"The woman pleaded with the villagers to help her, but they called her mad and accused her of killing her own baby. She swore at them and stormed into the forest to demand that the fairies return her child to her. She came back to the woods day after day, shouting, wailing, calling for anyone to help her. The forest heard her cries. The fairies heard her, too, and for her insolence, they cursed her. She would be doomed to wander the forest forever, snatching up any child she could find, although she would never find her own."*

"That's why the queen kidnaps kids who go into the forest," said Evie. "At least, that's what people say. Oscar Santos from school said she eats them when she realizes they're not hers, but Uncle Jim always says she turns them into wild animals."

"I don't think the real queen does either of those things," said Tinn. "I mean, she's scary. But I don't think she's murder-children scary. Well . . . probably not."

"It's so cool that you've actually met her. Do you think that the queen from all the stories is actually Fable's mom?"

"It can't be," said Tinn. "Old Jim has stories about the queen from when he was a kid, and he's old as dirt. Although . . ." His brow crinkled as he considered. "I guess she could be Fable's *grandma*."

"Keep reading," said Evie. "You're at the best part."

"For having the audacity to make demands of them, the fairies cruelly dubbed the woman a queen—a queen of nothing but dirt and shadows, Queen of the Deep Dark. The forest heard this, too, and it accepted the wretched woman as its own. When the hungry beasts of the forest eventually descended on the poor woman and tried to make a meal of her, the forest would not let them have her. The Witch of the

Wood had been born. A creature of fury and heartache, she let the curse seep deep inside her until it pulsed through her veins. To this day, her wails can be heard on the wind that carries through the trees, and death itself cannot tear her from the Deep Dark Forest. In lieu of her own daughter, the mad monarch became a mother to all the monsters of the forest, watching over the wild beasts as her own while swearing revenge on both humankind and fairies." Tinn turned the page, but the next entry was all about something called a *quinotaur.* Evie had sketched a picture of a bull with five horns.

"If you're right, then Fable's grandma sounds intense," said Evie. "I've never heard Uncle Jim say anything about a *new* queen, though. What do you think happened to the old one?"

Tinn shrugged. "I guess she probably died," he said.

They were quiet for a few paces.

"It's weird," said Evie, after a pause.

"What is?"

"I've always just thought of the queen as a monster, I guess. Not as somebody's grandma. Or somebody's mom. Or somebody."

"Everybody's somebody," said Tinn.

Evie nodded. "Everybody's somebody."

Tinn gently shut the journal and held it out for Evie. As she took it, her fingers closed around his and she smiled up at him for a moment. Tinn's brain felt numb.

Evie's head perked up. "Do you hear something?"

Tinn let go of the journal and peered into the leaves in front of them. They had long since lost sight of Fable and Cole, but he was fairly confident they were still on the right path. A quiet chittering came from the other side of the trees ahead, like a nest of quarreling squirrels. He held up a hand for Evie to wait as he inched closer.

No sooner had he poked his head around the trunk than the air erupted with a jabbering of voices. A whirlwind of twigs and rocks whipped around Tinn, scratching his arms and nicking the back of his neck.

He threw his hands over his face and staggered back. The noises subsided to a murmured growl, and Tinn peered out from behind his fingers.

A swarm of tiny figures surrounded him. The tallest of them was no larger than Tinn's shins; the smallest could have fit in his palm. Some were green, others brown or slate gray, and they looked as if their bodies had been carved from knobby sticks and rough stones. Several held miniature spears or pole-arms edged with ivory and jade. Tinn counted at least twenty of the creatures perched atop rocks, clinging to the tree bark, and forming ranks on the ground at Tinn's feet. They wore expressions that ranged from grumpy to murderous.

"Oh jeez," said Tinn. "I know what you are. Spriggans, right? Kull told me about you." He swallowed. "We're just passing through. We're not hurting anything."

One of the creatures, a stony spriggan with an uneven face liked cracked flint, stepped to the front of the swarm. "*Chttkkt-tchk-cht*," it said. Its brow cast a hard shadow over its steely eyes.

"Sorry, I don't speak . . . Spriggan. Spriggish?" Tinn held out his hands peaceably, and the figures tensed, tightening their grips on their weapons. "Wait! Wait, how about, um—" Tinn tried to remember the handful of phrases Kull had taught him in the strange, rolling, staccato language of the goblins. "*Good . . . daytime*," he managed in broken Goblish. "*Speak you . . . goblin . . . words?*"

The flinty spriggan's head turned to one side. It chittered something over its shoulder to one of its compatriots, and then looked back at Tinn. "*Bryll hobb'ns goblychth?*" it answered in a hoarse Goblish.

"Oh! You do!" said Tinn. "Shoot. I—erm—I don't. Not really. But I'm learning. I am one, see? I'm a goblin. A changeling—er, what's the word . . . *cudd—cuddio?*"

"*Bryll hobb'ns . . . cuddioll?*"

158

"Yeah. *Cuddioll*. That's it. I'm a changeling."

Flinty took a step closer. The spriggan's head bobbed up and down a fraction, sniffing Tinn, who glanced back at Evie. Her eyes were wide. "What's happening?" she asked.

"They don't like humans, but I think they're okay with goblins. I guess they're deciding if they believe that I am one or not."

"What about *me*?" Evie whispered.

Tinn did not have an answer. His hands were beginning to feel sweaty.

A low chatter spread through the other spriggans, and Flinty addressed Tinn again, unleashing a long string of Goblish syllables.

"What did he say?" breathed Evie.

"I—I don't know. I'm pretty sure I heard the word *now* at the end."

Flinty rolled his beady eyes. "Changeling," he rasped. "Change."

"You can speak English?" said Tinn.

"I can speak . . . enemy."

"We're not your enemies. I promise!"

"It smells goblin," said the spriggan. "It looks human."

"That's right! That's because I'm a"—Tinn glanced back at Evie—"because *we* are changelings. We're both goblins underneath, we just *look* like humans. Long story.

But you can smell that I'm actually goblin, so we're good here. Right?"

"Change."

Tinn cleared his throat. "The thing is, I sometimes have a hard time when somebody is watching or there's a lot of pressure and I—"

Flinty clicked his tongue once and the circle of figures surrounding Tinn tightened. The spriggans raised their blades, ready to attack.

"Change," Flinty repeated evenly.

Tinn took a deep breath. "Okay. I'll change, and then we'll go. Right? That's the deal?" He focused on Flinty's cracked, lopsided face. He could do this. He could look like a spriggan. A little marbling to his own skin and they would be on their way. He closed his eyes and imagined himself in a sea of magic, the waves lifting him up and down. *Don't try to control the waves*, he reminded himself. *Just help them take you to where you need to go.*

"Tinn?" Evie's voice behind him was shaking.

Look like stone. Look like stone, Tinn thought. But what then? Even if he could transform, would the furious little forest guardians really let them go without inspecting Evie, too? She had to be terrified right now. He should never have brought her. Even if, by some miracle, Tinn could

160

get his magic to work on cue and successfully prove he was a goblin—would that only mean that he would survive to watch them kill Evie right in front of him? He couldn't let that happen. His face felt tingly.

The spriggans began to chitter, and Tinn opened his eyes. Flinty was nodding at him, impressed. The weapons all around him lowered a fraction, and sinewy muscles relaxed. It had worked. Tinn put a hand to his cheek. It still felt soft and fleshy.

"You spoke truth," said Flinty, nodding. "Changeling."

"I told you," said Tinn. "We'll be out of your territory as soon as we can. We were just crossing through. So . . . goodbye?" Tinn held his breath.

Flinty eyed him for a moment, and then barked a command to the rest of the crew. They fell back to the base of the tree.

"Thanks," said Tinn. "We'll just be going, then. Come along, fellow changeling."

Evie did not waste a moment hurrying to his side.

"Goodbye, now," she said. "You're all doing a great job. Keep it up."

The hem of her skirt brushed close to a bright green spriggan whose torso looked like a vest of vibrant moss. The spriggan stiffened and squeaked.

"Keep walking," Tinn whispered.

Green chirped loudly to the mob, and the whole swarm sprang back to attention.

"Stop!" Flinty demanded.

Tinn bit his lip. They drew to a stop.

Flinty marched up close to Evie. He sniffed.

"Oh, don't mind her." Tinn tried to act nonchalant. His heart was beating so hard, he worried that the spriggans could hear it. "She's not as good at changing as I am. Takes her ages to do it."

"Looks human. Smells," Flinty growled, "*human.*"

Tinn's mouth continued to move silently as his brain tried frantically to figure out what words he could possibly put in it.

"You noticed," said Evie. "Thank you. Yes."

"That's just because—" Tinn began.

"—because I'm actually *more* advanced than he is," finished Evie.

Flinty cocked his head.

Tinn's mouth slowly closed.

"*He* still smells like a goblin," Evie explained. "But when you're an *advanced* changeling like me, you can make your scent change, too. Isn't that impressive? I'm getting rather good at human. It really helps when we're . . . erm . . . infiltrating the enemy."

The spriggans bubbled with chatter for several seconds as they discussed this new development. Tinn's whole body was tense. It wasn't going to work. They weren't going to buy it.

"Change," said Flinty.

Tinn readied his legs to run. If they were very, very lucky, they might make it out of the forest before the spriggans could do too much damage. He reached for Evie's hand, but hers had slid into the pocket of her dress.

"It might take me a second," Evie said.

What was she doing? Tinn's heart was racing.

Evie scrunched up her face in concentration. The spriggans eyed her dubiously. Tinn's throat felt dry. After an impossibly long moment, the vivid green spriggan at her feet squeaked again.

A series of jabbering chirps echoed around the swarm. Tinn glanced between Evie and the spriggans in confusion for a moment before the stench reached him. He nearly gagged, but managed to keep his composure.

"I'm doing *troll* now," Evie said. "Can you smell it?"

Several spriggans backed a few paces away, but the group as a whole appeared to have relaxed again.

"Needs practice," Flinty said. "Smells like ogre."

"You're absolutely right. This is much more like ogre than troll. I'll have to work on that." Evie nodded.

"Can do . . . elf?"

"Of course I can do elf," Evie said. "Elf is easy. Oh, but rotten luck. I should have started with that one. Ogre takes forever to wear off. And it's so overpowering. You understand, I'm sure."

Flinty gave a shrug that suggested he did, indeed, understand that the smell of ogre tended to linger.

"We really should be going now," Tinn said.

"It was very nice meeting you all," Evie added.

Flinty gave the smallest bob of his head, and the swarm of spriggans began to melt back into the underbrush.

Tinn held Evie's hand as they hurried on through the bracken. Neither of them spoke for several minutes.

"That was *brilliant*," Tinn breathed at last as the woods leveled out beneath them. "Wow. You smell *so* bad."

"Oh my gosh." Evie let go of his hand and emptied the clump of mashed wind blossoms out of her pocket. "Whoo. That was lucky is what it was. I can't believe it worked. That was so exciting. Spriggans! Can you believe I met real spriggans? What you did, though, transforming like that? For real? That was completely amazing! You didn't tell me you could do it so well."

"Oh. Thanks," said Tinn. "I just had to think about him really hard, and the magic kinda did the rest."

"Him?" Evie said.

"Yeah. I just kept my thoughts focused on the spriggan right in front of me so my face would look like his face. Wait. It did, didn't it?"

"Um. No." Evie gave Tinn a sort of lopsided smile. "Wait. You have to be thinking about something really hard to make yourself look like it?"

"Yeah, that's usually how it works. Why? What did I look like?"

"Well . . . me," said Evie. "For about ten seconds you looked just like me."

"Oh," said Tinn. His ears felt suddenly hot.

Evie took his hand in hers again. "Come on. I can see hills through the tree trunks up ahead. We're almost out of the forest."

Together, they made their way out of the shadows at last and toward the bright, clear daylight and the open hills.

SEVENTEEN

JACOB HILL'S DRILL SITE WAS A GRASSY FIELD nestled in a shallow dip between two hills. It was wide enough to squeeze in a decently sized baseball diamond, provided the outfielders didn't mind climbing up and down hills or clambering through wild growth. Right smack in the center of it, surrounded by sawdust and splinters, stood the enormous stump. It was four feet high, with roots as thick as Cole's waist and a top as broad across as the stage in Endsborough's auditorium.

Fable let out a long, slow breath. "Aw, man," she breathed. "*This* is why she's been so grumpy." Fable laid a hand on what remained of the Grandmother Tree.

The corpse of the tree lay in sections, stripped of its branches, at the northern side of the clearing. All around, shrubs and bushes had been ripped up, and a huge brush pile lay to one end of the field. Several more narrow tree stumps were also visible, low against the flattened terrain, and it was apparent Hill's efforts had pressed the forest line back at least fifty feet to make room for his grand project. As for the pump jack, all that remained now were a few standing timbers and a lot of debris.

Cole examined the remains of the equipment, picking his way carefully across the wreckage. Beams of wood had been snapped like toothpicks. Iron rods as thick as Cole's wrist had been twisted like paper clips and lay mangled in the dirt. Heavy cogs, like oversized clockwork, sat in a pile to the right. Three massive timbers and a couple of cross-beams remained intact, towering above them, although the structure leaned heavily to one side.

Cole heard Fable's footsteps scuff along the earth as she approached. "Are you okay?" he asked.

She scowled. "What *is* this?"

"I think it used to be a boring rig, for cutting into dirt and rocks and stuff," said Cole. "I've seen pictures."

"Whatever happened here, it doesn't look like it was very boring," said Fable.

"Why was he digging so close to the forest in the first

167

place?" Cole wondered. "Wouldn't it have been easier to just do it up by the old farmhouse?"

Fable shrugged. "I don't know," she said. "But the forest is not happy. This is definitely where it was sending me."

"Are the trees finally talking to you?" Cole asked.

Fable wobbled a hand from side to side. "It's less like words and more like annoying pokes in my tummy. Not as helpful as you might think. But now that we're here, it feels obvious. *I'm* not happy, either."

Cole's eyes dropped to the ground. "It looks like you and the trees aren't the only ones who aren't happy," he said. He took a step back and Fable followed his gaze.

The two of them stood on either side of a massive footprint in the soil. Pressed into the freshly churned dirt was one broad pad with five clearly defined toes. The indentation was as big as Cole's mattress. He could have lain down inside the thing and still had room to spare.

"Giants," said Cole in an awed whisper.

"If there are giants in my forest," said Fable, "then they are the *best* hiders *ever.*"

"Shh, do you hear someone?" Cole hunched down. "Shoot. The grown-ups must be here already."

The two of them ducked behind what was left of the drilling equipment.

"Just this way," came the voice of Jacob Hill. "Here,

ladies and gentlemen. We were standing right here when the brute lumbered off into the trees."

Cole peeked out between the spokes of an oversized wooden cog.

Hill was leading the way down the hillside toward the field, followed by a handful of townspeople. Amos Washington, who was near the front, gave a low whistle. "Is that your rig, Mr. Hill?"

"It was," Hill grunted. His eyes darted to the tree line every few seconds. "What's left of the drill is lodged in the dirt over there. Mind your step, sir. You're standing right in the middle of the proof we were looking for."

Mr. Washington glanced down and then stepped gingerly out of the enormous footprint.

"This is one heck of a sight." He shook his head. "I've seen a lot of strange stuff around here, but I've never seen anything that could do this."

"We have no way of knowing if it's authentic, of course," said Helen Grouse. "I'm sorry, Mr. Hill. I don't mean to be distrustful, but—"

"No offense taken. I wouldn't believe me either," Hill said. "It's mad."

"Where did it come from?" asked Mr. Washington.

"Heck if I know." Hill waved at the forest line. "I was more concerned with getting out of here in one piece.

You're welcome to follow the tracks for yourselves if you like. I'll keep to the open ground, if it's all the same to you."

Cole held as still as he could as Mr. Washington stepped past the kids' hiding spot, followed by Mrs. Grouse and a handful of other inquisitive townsfolk. Fable put a hand on his shoulder and pointed. Cole glanced back up.

Annie Burton had just joined the gathering in the clearing. "Oh my." She blew out a long puff of air as she surveyed the damaged machine and the freakish footprints.

"It's a lot to take in, I know," said Hill.

"Pardon me, Mr. Hill," she said. "There are an awful lot of stumps in this area. Did you cut down all these trees recently?"

"Yes, ma'am. Finished the big one off only yesterday."

Annie cringed and drew in a sharp breath.

Mr. Hill appeared to take her alarm for admiration. "Yup. It took four of us to bring it down." He nodded at all the felled timber around the field. "Made arrangements with the mill to sell most of it. Nice to get back a small piece of my initial investment."

"But if the trees came all the way up to here," Annie pressed, "doesn't that mean this area was technically a part of the Wild Wood?"

Cole felt Fable's hand tighten on his shoulder.

"Certainly not," Hill replied. "Don't worry. I took

meticulous measurements, followed the property lines precisely."

"Did he"—Fable's voice was a harsh whisper—"did he really cut a whole corner off my forest just to draw a stupid line?" Her nostrils flared.

"Shh." Cole put a finger to his lips, but Fable's scowl was deepening.

"This whole endeavor has been no easy feat," Hill continued. "I kept chalking it up to bad luck—but it's all beginning to make sense now. Compasses suddenly spinning for no reason, the earth shaking—and now actual monsters? I really don't know how you people have lived side by side with this Wild Wood for so long without doing something about it."

A few of the townspeople who remained milling about the site murmured in agreement. "I've always said we shouldn't be tolerating the little stuff," Mr. Fenerty said. "Said it a hundred times. You leave milk out for a pixie one night, let a hob root through your garbage the next, it's a slippery slope to goblins and trolls and giants, no mistake."

Hill shook his head. "It's madness to allow such dangerous beasts to live so close to people at all!" He threw up his hands. "Madness!"

"*Allow* them to?" Fable glared.

"Shh," Cole whispered.

171

"*Allow* them to?" Fable repeated at full volume. Her face was flushed as she stood upright, emerging from her hiding spot. Cole put his hands over his eyes as she stalked out from behind the wreckage. Hill jumped visibly as she emerged and nearly lost his footing. "*They* were here *first*," said Fable. "*They* allow *people* to live so close to *them*."

Annie gaped. "What on earth—Fable?" She peered a little closer. "Cole Thomas Burton, I can see you back there!"

Cole shot Fable a dark glance and sighed as he stood up, too. "Hi, Mom."

"I *told* you to stay put!" she said.

"Yeah. But, in our defense, you know we never do," he said. "So I didn't think you really expected it this time."

Annie rubbed her temples. "And where is your brother?"

"He should be here any minute," said Cole.

"You boys are hard enough to keep track of when you stay together," Annie grumbled. "This is serious! You know how dangerous it can be so far from town. You are in *so* much trouble."

"You can't entirely blame the children," Hill said, poking about the broken pieces of his pump jack. "*Nobody* in this town seems to take the threat seriously."

"Please, Mr. Hill." Annie turned to the man. "We take the dangers of the forest very seriously around here. There's not a child in town who isn't raised to respect the borders of—"

"But you shouldn't *have* to! That's the point—it's tragic!" Hill picked up a broken iron rod about three feet long and waved it like a baton at the surrounding forest. "The Wild Wood is a danger! What's the point of having all this beautiful wilderness right in your own backyard if you can't even let your children run about without fearing for their lives?" Hill said.

"Who says wilderness needs to have a *point*?" Fable grumbled. "It's *wilderness. That's* the point."

"The man ain't wrong," said Old Jim Warner, coming in at the back of the group. He had a rifle over one shoulder, and a grim expression on his face. "People lose themselves in that forest. Been tellin' folks for years. There's some powerful dangerous magic in them woods. Things that would make grown men cry." He shifted the rifle to both hands, eyeing the shadows of the forest soberly.

"Do be careful with that thing," said Annie. "There are children present."

"I ain't fixing to shoot anything I don't have to." Jim sniffed. "Just prefer the forest to be afraid of me, and not the other way around." He punctuated his statement by aiming his barrel steadily in the direction of the tree line.

The Queen of the Deep Dark crossed through the woods with her head held high. She did not enjoy knowing that the ancient guardians of the forest—of *her* forest—were meeting in secret to discuss her affairs behind her back. It was fine, she told herself. Let them discuss whatever matters they liked with whomever they wished. When the talking was done, she would still be queen.

As she neared the northwestern limits of the Wild Wood, she slowed. The forest ached. The sound of the mighty Grandmother Tree crashing to the earth echoed in the back of her mind. With it hummed the irritating doubt that perhaps the spriggans were not entirely wrong. Had she been neglecting her duties? She crushed the thought with a mental heel, but it crawled off into a dark corner of her mind to bide its time.

Ahead of her, the queen heard voices. Her eyes narrowed, and she stepped closer. There were children in her forest. A boy—one of the twins that Fable was so fond of—and a girl she had never seen before. They had not yet noticed her, so she closed in on them silently, keeping to the shadows as she moved. As the trees began to thin, still more voices pierced the air. Adults this time. An old man. A woman. Was that Annie Burton?

The queen scowled. A movement to the north caught her eye. Even as the boy and girl picked their way slowly out of the woods to her left, someone else was stomping into them to her right.

"Watch your step, Mrs. Grouse," a man's voice said.

Humans! There were humans all around her—in her forest! The audacity! The impudence! This was completely unacceptable. Didn't they have entire cities of their own to ruin? What did they think they were doing?

Another voice carried through the branches, and the queen halted.

"The forest is fine just the way it is!" Fable said. Her voice had come from just beyond the edge of the tree line. She was outside of the Wild Wood.

Fable had left the forest. Whatever this was, her daughter was a part of it.

That child was in so much trouble.

Jacob Hill leaned on the iron rod like a cane and shook his head. "I'm just saying, what good is a natural resource if its *resources* can never be tapped?" he said. "I've heard a lot of local legends: former lumber workers who refuse to touch another tree, quarry workers who are afraid to crack a rock. They're all *true*, aren't they?" The sound of twigs crackling pulled Hill's attention away and he spun toward the forest. "What was that?"

Annie stepped in front of Cole. "Stay behind me," she said.

Something was emerging from the woods.

Old Jim leveled his rifle at the noise. Gradually, two figures stepped out of the darkness. He dropped the barrel at once. "Evie?" he said. "What in tarnation?"

"Tinn!" yelled Annie. "You kids cut through the *forest*? What on earth were you thinking?"

"Sorry, Mom," Tinn said. "It was all my idea. It's my fault. I'm an idiot."

She opened her mouth to agree, but another noise brought her attention to the edge of the woods again, just a little farther north.

Jim raised his rifle again, but lowered it almost at once. It was only Mr. Washington's group returning.

"Find anything interesting?" said Old Jim.

"Afraid so," said Washington. "The tracks are fake."

"What?" Hill said.

"Either that or Hill's giant magically flew away." Washington shrugged. "We followed them in a ways. They just stop completely about thirty feet past the edge of the trees."

"You lost the trail?" Hill said.

Washington shook his head. "Of a sixty-foot giant? My old man raised me hunting rabbits. I know how to find a trail. Like I said, it just stops."

"But how?" Hill put a hand through his dusty hair.

"Why don't *you* tell *us*?" Washington said.

"Me?"

"It does look awful sketchy." Mrs. Grouse crossed her arms.

"You think *I* did this? You can see what that thing did to my drill! Why would I destroy my own equipment? Hurt my own crew?"

"Come on, boys," said Annie. "Let's all go home."

"Wait!" Hill shouted, pointing into the woods. "Look! There!"

"Let it go, man," said Helen Grouse.

"No! I saw something! Just there!"

With a sigh, Old Jim raised his rifle one more time and peered into the gloom.

"Shoot it!" Hill shouted.

"Shoot what?" Jim answered. "I'm not going to fire blind into the woods." But even as he said it his eyes locked on to the faintest shudder of motion within the shadows of the forest. Instinctively, his thumb drew back the hammer. For a fraction of a moment, he saw what might have been a figure clad in a long, shaggy cloak.

"If you won't, then let me do it!" Hill grabbed for the rifle and tried to yank it from Jim's grasp.

"Enough!" cried Annie Burton. "Stop that before somebody gets—"

The gun went off with a *boom*.

A *single shot of lead and brass*. The queen's eyes hung open as the echo of the gunshot faded away like ripples in a pond. Shaking, she reached a hand up to brush the spot with her fingers. Mangled splinters splayed around a small hole in the tree beside her as if a flower had just bloomed on its trunk.

She took a deep breath, her whole body shaking. The queen was not hurt. She was not afraid. The queen was livid.

EIGHTEEN

Fable took quiet footsteps as she eased herself back into the woods a few minutes later. Behind her, the townspeople had already begun plodding back down the human road, grumbling and whispering as they went. The sun had slid well beyond midday, but maybe if Fable hurried, her mother would still be waiting for her in the glen. She was bound to be angry that Fable was late for her lesson. Fable skipped over a patch of vines and pushed through a curtain of hanging leaves. Her mother was waiting on the other side.

Fable blinked.

The queen did not.

"Hi," said Fable. "So. You . . . saw?"

"I saw."

"There were reasons," Fable began.

"There always are."

"Tinn and Cole were lost."

"Tinn and Cole"—the queen repeated the names through gritted teeth—"are trouble. You are not to see those boys again. Or anyone else from the village."

Fable gaped. "What?" she said. "But they're my friends."

"They are *not* your friends," said the queen. "*People* are never your friends, Fable. People don't belong in our forest at all. They are bad men. They bring axes and saws . . . and *gunfire*, Fable. This is my own fault. I have allowed the humans too much freedom in our domain. I need to be more firm—and that starts with *you*."

"Mama. Please, listen . . ."

"Did you know that they brought *strangers* into the forest?"

"Who? Evie? Evie isn't strangers," said Fable. "She's my friend, too."

"*None* of them are your friends!" the queen yelled.

Fable's chest hurt. She clenched her fists.

"And *you*," the queen continued, tempering her voice like hardened steel, "are not just some silly human girl who can skip and laugh and play whenever you like. You have responsibilities. You need to be ready. You are important, Fable. You are the future queen of this forest, and it is long past time that you began to act like it."

"Maybe I don't want to be important!" Fable burst. "Maybe I'd rather be a silly human girl than grow up to be a horrible, rotten queen of a bunch of trees!"

"Fable—"

"No! You want me to be like *you*," Fable yelled, "but I'm never going to be like you! You're awful and everybody hates you!" Fable had never spoken to her mother this way before. She felt dizzy, like she was yelling while running through a twisting tunnel. Her face felt hot—but she couldn't stop, not now that the dam had broken. "I don't want to be queen like you, I don't want to do magic like you, and I don't want to be mean and lonely for my whole life like you!" All around her, the foliage bent and leaned away. The trunks of the pine trees groaned and crackled. "I am *never* going to be the stupid queen of your stupid forest! You can keep it!"

The forest was unnaturally silent as both of them breathed for several seconds, and then Fable turned away from her mother without asking permission and stalked off through the woods. She could feel her heartbeat in her ears.

"Wait . . ." her mother called.

"And they *are* my friends!" Fable did not look back.

Fable did not speak to her mother again for the rest of the day. She did her best to avoid crossing paths, but for all the acres the Wild Wood covered, she could not seem to escape her. She caught sight of a familiar bearskin cloak watching over her as she picked berries that evening, and spotted familiar hazel eyes in the leaves as she tossed pebbles into the Oddmire.

The following day, she glanced up from getting a drink in a stream to find the queen watching from the opposite bank, her face inscrutable as always. Fable was wearing the dress that Annie had given her, if only because she knew her mother would not approve. It had already grown dingy from wear, and it caught in the branches when she was climbing, but it was still fancier by far than her usual dust-brown canvas frock.

"Fable," her mother said. "We need to talk."

Fable folded her arms and stomped away in the opposite direction without giving her mother the satisfaction of a response.

On the third day, Fable was sitting on the banks of the Oddmire with Squidge. To distract herself, she had invented a little game in which she poked two sticks into the thick gunk of the mire—one for herself and one for the hedgehog—and then tried to guess which one would sink or topple first. So far, both had remained upright for several minutes. The mire was especially thick today.

Fable considered using compel to speed things along, but if one of the sticks accidentally turned into a chipmunk or something, she didn't want to have to get her dress all mucky pulling it out.

A *boom* like a thunderclap shook the air, and the trees around her shuddered. Fable's attention snapped toward Endsborough. Over the trees, a cloud of smoke billowed into the sky.

Fable was on her feet in a flash. "Stay here, Squidge."

The hedgehog watched as Fable pelted away. Behind her, both sticks sank slowly into the mire.

As Fable neared the town, she could hear muffled shouting. Something was happening in the city. She wanted desperately to know what was going on, but she knew she shouldn't cross the border. Her mother had expressly forbidden her from seeing anyone from town, and she had already crossed so many lines.

Somebody screamed.

Fable's jaw clenched. She glanced left and right into the trees around her. There was no sign anywhere of a furry brown cloak or a pair of steely, disapproving eyes.

Fable crept to the forest's edge and the little stream that divided the forest from the town. She could hear more voices now. A pair of men in coveralls hurried down a dusty street toward the source of the excitement. There was something else, too. She sniffed the air. It was sharp and bitter, like the smell in the air after Old Jim Warner had fired that gun. A column of smoke continued to pour upward into the sky.

In the distance, a voice shouted: "Help!"

Fable glanced behind her one last time, took a deep breath, and then hopped over the burbling water into Endsborough.

NINETEEN

T<small>INN AND</small> C<small>OLE COULD FEEL THE HEAT OF THE</small> blaze from twenty feet away. Smoke stung their eyes. Annie Burton held the boys' shoulders as all three of them stared, openmouthed, at the inferno. The explosion had blown out the windows in the ground floor of Fenerty's Stationery and Paper Goods, and the flames had been quick to make their way upstairs. Bits of burning paper rained down like hellish ticker tape confetti as the fire punched through a second-story window to wave at the horrified onlookers.

Several dozen townsfolk were already passing buckets of water from the creek that ran behind the Lucky Pig up to the burning building and back again to be refilled.

"I'm going to help," Annie said. "You two—stay back. I am not kidding this time." The twins nodded solemnly as their mother fell into line with the bucket brigade.

They could hear the fire station bell clanging away. Cole and Tinn had seen them roll out the steam pumper before. It was an impressive thing, but it took several minutes to get its boiler going and get the horses hitched up to the front. Cole peered up the dusty road, waiting to see them when they came around the corner.

Endsborough was alive with activity. Townsfolk bustled from door to door, eager to inform their neighbors of the chaos. Albert Townshend nearly tripped over his own feet carrying a sloshing mop bucket up the road. Old Mrs. Stewart had come out to watch the excitement from the comfort of her rocking chair.

A motion just up the street caught Cole's attention and he blinked in surprise. The air was hot and dry, and it made his eyes water—but he could have sworn he had seen a lithe figure with a mess of dark curls slipping along the wall.

Fable held her breath. She had snuck into town just long enough to find out what the heck was going on, and she would sneak back out again as soon as she was satisfied. In and out. Nobody even needed to know she had ever been here.

She quickstepped across the dusty road and ducked behind a barrel of dry goods. On the other side of the barrel, she could hear the rhythmic creak of a rocking chair.

There was a burst of noise as a door opened across the street and a crowd of men with sloshing buckets and thick blankets emerged. Fable glanced left and right, and then hopped hastily inside the barrel to hide. Her heart pounded. She felt excited, but also silly—it wasn't as if any of those men cared one fig about her. The hiding spot was full of hazelnuts, which rattled as she sank into them. She waited as the sound of voices faded away.

Gradually, Fable realized the rhythmic creaking of the rocking chair had stopped, too. There was a little wooden groan and then the shuffle of footsteps. *Don't look inside the barrel*, Fable thought, tensing as if sheer force of will could conceal her.

A wrinkled face appeared in the circle of light above her. "Hello, young lady," said the woman. Her eyes twinkled. She appeared neither startled nor angry to find a child nestled among the nuts.

"Hi." Fable smiled weakly up at the face.

"Have we met?" the woman asked, squinting as she surveyed the girl in the barrel.

"Um. I don't think so," said Fable.

There was a pause as the woman considered her.

"I'm . . . not supposed to be here," said Fable.

"I should think not," the woman agreed. "You're the wrong shape entirely for a hazelnut."

"I'm hiding."

"I won't tell," said the woman with a wink.

The hazelnuts shifted slightly as Fable relaxed. "I'm Fable," she said.

"Hello, Fable," said the woman. "My name is Margaret."

"I like your hair," said Fable. "I like how it's all white and sort of swooshy."

The lady gave a little chuckle and the creases around her eyes deepened. "It wasn't always so white. It used to be as dark as yours, if you can believe it. Are you sure we haven't met?"

"I'm not from here."

"Mm. You must remind me of somebody I used to know." The woman settled back into her chair as Fable climbed gingerly back out of the barrel.

"I'm sorry I sat on your hazelnuts," said Fable. "I didn't take any. Promise."

The woman looked out over the street. "You'll miss a whole lot, you know, hiding away." She took a deep breath. "Quite the show lately. The iceman let some children ride on the back of his cart on Saturday. I assumed that was the highlight of the week. But then there was all the excitement with that Mr. Hill fellow a few days ago, and I thought for sure that was the topper. The whole town has been talking about monsters and giants ever since. But now here's this."

"I don't like Mr. Hill," said Fable. "He cut down a tree my mama really liked."

"That grand old oak? I was sad to hear about that, too." The woman looked out over the rooftops and fidgeted with the end of her necklace.

"Why were *you* sad about it?" said Fable. "It wasn't *your* tree. It was a *forest* tree."

"Mm." The woman's eyes sparkled as she looked at Fable. "I was a little girl once," she said at last, "if you can believe it. Long before the white hair and the wrinkles, before I got married and moved away from my daddy's farm. I was Maggie Roberson back then." She smiled and reached behind her neck to unclasp her necklace. She held it out for Fable to see. "I know you young people call me *Old Mrs. Stewart* these days. I don't mind. Everybody seems young lately. But I keep a bit of little Maggie with me still."

The necklace was nothing more than a thin chain that ended in a polished green stone. Fable held out a hand, and the woman let it rest in her palm. The gem was smooth and almost clear enough to see through—cloudy white with a spray of dark green veins spreading out from the center. It was pretty, but Fable had seen countless like it. The narrow path leading up to her grandmother's old cabin was lined with scores of them.

"I used to have an imaginary friend," the woman said, watching Fable's fingers as they turned the stone around and around. "I just called her *my lady*. She lived in the woods behind our farm when I was very young, and whenever I went picking berries or playing near the forest's edge, I would invent songs to cheer her up."

"Why did your imaginary friend need cheering up?"

"You know, I can't for the life of me remember," said the old woman. "But that is an excellent question."

"I'm good at questions," Fable said.

The woman smiled. "One day I made up a song about finding rubies and emeralds and buried pirate treasure, and the next morning, a whole pile of these was waiting for me in my favorite tree."

"Are they valuable?"

"In their way." She smiled and held out her hand. Fable returned the necklace, and the woman slid the chain back around her neck. "Moss agate. They used to say it was good luck for gardens or babies or new beginnings. I scooped them out of that old oak tree and carried them up the hill in my skirts. My brothers and I spent a whole day hiding them around our field. We thought it might make the crops grow better. This one I kept for myself, though. It reminds me to have courage to try something new from time to time."

A tingle went up Fable's back. "You found those in the Grandmother Tree?"

"The *Grandmother Tree*? I like that. Yes, I found them in that old oak. My brothers never believed me, but it's true. Such a shame about that tree. It was my favorite place when I was young. I sang a lot of songs to my lady from its branches." She smiled wistfully. "I must have had such an imagination back then. She was so real to me. I can almost see her eyes."

Fable stared at the stone around the woman's neck.

"You're sure we haven't met?" the woman said. "It's just that you are so familiar."

"I'm pretty sure," said Fable.

"Hm. Never mind. I do believe your friends are here, little hazelnut."

Fable looked up. "Huh?"

Tinn and Cole came sliding to a stop in front of Mrs. Stewart's porch. "Fable!" said Tinn. "When did you get here?"

Fable glanced back at the old woman. "I should go. But

it was very nice to meet you, Maggie. Thank you for telling me about your lady."

The old woman smiled politely, and Fable hopped off the porch to join the boys.

"What's going on?" she said when they had ushered her half a block up the road.

"The paper store just blew up!" Cole said as they rounded the corner. "And that's not all. It's been nuts. Mostly little stuff: chicken coops keep getting unlocked, windows have gotten broken all over town, and there's been weird noises during the night. People are getting really mad."

"They're saying gremlins spooked the post office horses this morning," said Tinn.

"Gremlins?" said Fable. "But gremlins don't even live on this side of the Wild Wood. They're butts, but they almost never go out of their way for a prank."

"It looks like they made the trip," said Tinn. "There were claw marks and everything."

They turned the corner and the stationery store came into view at the end of the block, flames dancing from the windows and smoke pouring into the sky. The kids scurried out of the way as the fire brigade howled past in its shiny pumper, bells clanging. The firefighters ground to a stop in front of the burning store and raced around, fiddling with hoses and big brass knobs. Fable couldn't help but think that now would be a really good time to have an invisible brain-hand that could put out fires.

"Old Jim thinks it was fire salamanders," said Tinn. "And people are starting to listen to him."

Fable sniffed the smoky air. Salamanders did occasionally get overexcited around this time of year. She had helped her mother control a few minor forest fires near the southern bend of the mire, where they liked to nest. But something wasn't right.

"I don't think it was salamanders," she said. She sniffed more deeply, and her nose crinkled. "I know what salamander fire smells like, and it's not this."

"Well," said Cole, lowering his voice, "whatever it is, *everybody* is talking about it, so be extra careful. Being from the Wild Wood will *not* make you friends in town today."

The heat of the burning building rolled over them from the far end of the block. The roar and crackle of the fire mixed with urgent shouts. The firefighters had taken up a position right in front, and with a whoosh the pumper let out a stream of water that punched through the flames on the ground floor.

"What makes everybody so sure all this stuff was done by forest folk?" Fable said.

Tinn and Cole glanced at each other.

193

"I mean," said Tinn. "This is the kind of stuff they do."

"Who's *they*?" Fable's scowl deepened. "*I'm* forest folk," she said. "And this is *not* what I do. This isn't normal at all."

"I didn't mean it like that," said Tinn.

"This wasn't salamanders," Fable said. "And I don't know if I believe it was gremlins, either. Did anybody actually *see* gremlins spook the horses? Has anyone caught *any* actual creatures from my forest running amok?"

"Well, no," said Cole.

"See? Then maybe it's just . . . maybe it's—"

Before Fable could think of a theory to replace the forest folk invasion, half a dozen townspeople hurried across the street in front of them. Old Jim was keeping a steady gait at the back of the pack, his rifle slung over one shoulder and an empty wire trap under his arm. Beside him, Evie was jogging to keep up.

"Evie!" called Tinn. "What's happening now?"

"You didn't hear?" she said. "They *caught* one!"

TWENTY

MR. ZERVOS' SHOP WAS NOT FAR FROM THE
burning stationery store. As the children approached, they
could see fifteen or sixteen townspeople already crowding
around the front window, leaning over one another's shoulders and craning their necks to peer inside.

"Mr. Zervos found it," Evie said with breathless excitement. "It was already inside when he opened the door. He
said he heard the sound of glass breaking, and *whoom*! It
flew right up in his face!"

"What did?" Fable asked.

"An itty-bitty person with blue skin and wings like a
dragonfly."

"It's true!" said Mr. Zervos, emerging from the huddle around the window. His eyes were wide. "It was flying around my head, waving tiny arms and buzzing like a cicada. It's still in there somewhere, smashing up furniture and knocking things off of shelves. I've heard stories, of course, but I've never seen anything like it up close."

"That sounds like a pixie," said Fable. She pushed her way between onlookers and shielded her eyes from the sun with her hand as she peered in through the glass. "But why would there be a pixie all the way out here?" Evie squeezed in beside her, and the boys joined them on either side. The front room was a mess, with beef jerky strewn across the counter, magazines torn to shreds, and tin cans rolling across the floor, but the creature itself was nowhere to be seen. A loud crash and a thump issued from somewhere in the back of the shop, and a white cloud of flour began to descend like gently settling snow.

"Smart girl. It *does* sound like a pixie," said a voice behind them. Old Jim Warner shoved his way forward. "Outta the way, folks. Somebody's got to roll up their shirtsleeves and deal with this thing instead of standing around gawking. Looks like it's me, as usual."

"What are you going to do to it?" asked Tinn.

"You're *not* shooting it," said Fable, squaring off between Jim and the front door of the shop. "No guns."

196

"Of course I ain't shooting it." Old Jim snorted. "Do I look like a crazy person to you, kid?"

"I don't know," said Fable soberly. "What does a crazy person look like?"

"Not like me," said Old Jim. "For example, I am not about to go firing a rifle in the middle of a busy town to try and hit a moving target the size of a golf ball. I do, however, have this trap"—he plopped the wire cage down on the step—"and a secret weapon." He gave Evie a wink.

Faces peered over shoulders to see the old man's secret weapon. Evie pulled a dented tin can out of the pocket of her dress. The label read Sweetened Condensed Milk.

"Give it here, kiddo," said Old Jim.

He handed the rifle to Mr. Zervos, who pointed it cautiously at the dirt while Old Jim got to work. He pulled a penknife from his back pocket and popped open the can, then poured a spoonful of sweetened milk into a shallow metal cup at the back of the trap. He gently positioned the mechanism, and when he was done, he picked the whole thing up with one hand and cracked open the door with the other. He slid the cage inside, ever so gently so as not to trip the spring, and then shut the door with a click.

"And now, we wait." He peered into the broad picture window. Mr. Zervos and all of the others stared into the window, too. Nothing moved. A muffled clatter issued from somewhere in the back storage room, then all was still again.

"Come on," whispered Cole. "Let's go around back and see if we can see anything." Tinn, Fable, and Evie followed him to the rear of the building. They scooted past the trash bins and clambered up onto the loading dock. There was a single dusty window, and the four of them crowded around it. Evie stepped up on a wooden milk crate to get a better look.

"I don't see a pixie," said Cole. "Man. It got flour every-where, though."

"Hang on," said Tinn. "Look at the window."

"Where do you think we're looking?" said Cole.

"No, not inside it. I mean look at it. The window frame is all scratched and cracked, and the latch is broken. It looks like somebody broke in."

"You think this is how the pixie got in there in the first place?" said Evie.

"We don't even know for sure it's a pixie," whispered Fable.

THWAP!

All four of them jumped as a miniature blue woman thudded against the window. She was only about three inches tall, with a wingspan twice as broad. She bonked her shoulder against the window a few times, looking confused and agitated, her delicate wings fluttering like a moth's, tiny fists pinging uselessly against the glass. And then, as quickly as she had appeared, she was gone again into the depths of the shop.

"Definitely a pixie," said Fable. "Angry, angry pixie."

"Oh my gosh, oh my gosh, oh my gosh!" Evie nearly tottered backward off of her milk crate.

"She's stuck in there," said Cole.

"If she was strong enough to break the frame to get in, then why doesn't she just bust back out again?" said Tinn.

Fable leaned forward and sniffed the glass. "Guys. I smell pixies all the time. I mean . . . not on purpose—they don't like it when you smell them on purpose—but I know their scent. This window does *not* smell like pixies." She regarded the pixie-shaped imprint the creature had left in the thin layer of flour on the inside of the glass. "At least not on the outside. I imagine the inside probably does now."

"If she didn't break in, then someone must have *let* her in there," said Cole.

There was a muffled *snap*, and voices cheered from the front of the building.

The kids vaulted off the loading dock and raced around to the other side of the shop just in time to see Old Jim step out the door with the rattling cage in his hand. The noise coming from the trap was something between the drone of an insect and the piteous mewl of a cat.

"And that, boys and girls," Old Jim said, "is how you catch a pixie."

The creature's wail grew louder and louder until she slammed herself against the wires with a shriek. A boy a few years younger than the twins jumped and fell over backward. Even the adults in the crowd gasped. One woman held tight to the cross hanging from her neck and mumbled a prayer. Mr. Zervos looked pale.

"We hear you, you little pest," Old Jim said, giving the cage a rattle that sent the pixie stumbling off her feet.

"She's frightened," said Fable. "Stop shaking her!"

"Kid, this critter might be small, but she just went through that store like a tornado," said Old Jim. "She's no wilting flower. Don't let that pretty face fool you. She would bite your nose clean off given half a chance. And she wouldn't feel bad about it. Trust me. She can handle a jiggle." The pixie snarled at Old Jim, and he chuckled.

"She doesn't want to bite noses off. She just wants to go home," said Fable. "Can't you see that?"

"I know what I'm dealing with," Old Jim grunted. "I've been dealing with nonsense out of that forest my whole life."

Fable's lips tightened. All around them, anxious murmurs were making their way through the crowd.

"Did you see its teeth?" someone whispered.

"Lord Almighty."

"Not so close, Timothy! Stay away from it!"

Jim set the cage down on the step and signaled for Mr. Zervos to hand him his rifle back. "I guess I'll take our unwanted guest back home with me and decide what to do with her there. I bet my Evie can get some real nice drawings out of—hey!" Old Jim spun around so fast that Mr. Zervos almost dropped the rifle before he could hand it to him. "Get away from that cage!" Old Jim yelled.

"No," said Fable. And she opened the trap.

"Fable, wait!" said Evie, a moment too late.

Someone screamed. The whole crowd leapt back, and a woman toward the front tripped over her own legs and fell. Old Jim threw his hands over his face as a blue blur exploded out of the opening and careened over the rooftops until it vanished into the trees beyond.

"You wanted to know what crazy looks like?" Old Jim barked. "*That!*"

"I was right," said Fable. "She went home."

"If all that miniature monster wanted was to be *home*,"

growled Old Jim, "then what was she doing way out *here* in the first place?"

Fable had no answer.

Mr. Zervos helped the fallen woman to her feet, and all around them faces looked visibly shaken.

"Brazen," somebody said.

"You think that thing caused the paper fire, too?" another voice mused.

"Not big enough to be the one left those marks on the stable," added a third.

"What about the broken pots in my garden?"

Fable tried to ignore them. Her brow crinkled. Smashed drills, frightened horses, burned-up buildings—admittedly, there were plenty of creatures in the wood capable of this kind of mayhem, but there was no way that one little pixie was the cause. The poor thing couldn't even open a window.

"You've got your grumpy face on," said Cole. "What are you thinking about?"

"Okay," she said with a sigh. "So, there *might* be some creatures from my forest running amok. What I can't figure out is *why.*"

TWENTY-ONE

KALLRA WAS GONE. HER REFLECTING POOL SAT still and empty, disturbed only by the occasional gentle wind. The queen stood over it anyway, her cloak brushing the soft grass at the water's edge. She gazed into the glistening pool, wishing for answers she knew it would not surrender.

She closed her eyes. In her mind, the Grandmother Tree came crashing to earth for the hundredth time, and with it came those spiteful words: *She does nothing*.

She did not mean to think about it, but it was like a hand brushing over a scar. It was as if she had allowed a piece of herself to be lopped off. And she had done nothing.

A piercing buzz broke the stillness of the morning and drew the queen away from the glittering waters and her own thoughts. She brushed aside the curtain of leaves and emerged back into the thick of the Wild Wood.

Not far off, a cloud of angry pixies swarmed a grumbling bogle. He was a grubby thing, his hair coarse and thin, his hide a blotchy gray. He didn't even bother batting the pixies away as he went about plucking toadstools from their ring one by one and stuffing them into a tattered sack on his side. The pixies screamed and bombarded the creature with scratches and kicks and bites, none of which fazed the bogle.

"What do you think you are doing?" said the queen. The bogle glanced up, unimpressed.

"*They* wasn't eating them," he grunted, gesturing at the screaming figures around his head.

"You know perfectly well that fairy circles denote sacred ground. Step out of that ring at once and return their property."

For several long seconds, the bogle just stared at the queen, scowling, his eyes half-lidded but sharp. She found something in his expression disquieting. For a fraction of a second, his gaze flickered upward, and then back to the queen. She looked up. On a tree branch hanging over them perched a single pale brown spriggan. The figure watched in stony silence through narrowed eyes. She noted the tiny pouch hanging from the creature's neck—a war satchel. Her shoulders tensed.

The last thing she needed with spriggans literally hanging over her head and humans pushing their limits on all sides was a drawn-out conflict between forest factions.

The bogle watched her expression through keen, beady eyes as circling pixies screeched. The queen felt the blood rush to her face. She was being tested. Here, in her own forest, she was being tested by a grubby little bogle!

She arched an eyebrow. It was an expression that had cowed far more dangerous beasts in the past. She held her breath. If the bogle did not relent, she did not want to think about what she would need to do to him to regain the fear and respect she had once held over the Wild Wood. As if coming to this thought himself, the bogle finally took two very slow, deliberate steps out of the ring and turned his filthy bag upside down. The toadstools landed in the grass with a quiet *plut-plut-plut*. He did this without taking his eyes off of the queen, and then he gave her an exaggerated bow.

The queen breathed.

"Wise choice," said a voice from behind them both.

With a flash of red cardinal feathers, a familiar weathered top hat peeked out of the ferns, followed by an even more weathered face.

"Thief King. You have been spending an awful lot of time away from Hollowcliff of late."

"Just keepin' a weathered eye on things, Yer Majesty."

"Are you? Then tell me," said the queen, "what exactly is happening in my forest? Something has changed. I don't like it."

"Cogs are turnin'," Nudd said. "Big ones."

"Your weathered eye leaves a lot to be desired."

Nudd shrugged. "My goblins is on hand ta help turn the tides if need be," he said.

"If you want to be helpful, then you could try to talk *them*"—she gestured up at the spriggan still perched above them—"out of getting everyone overexcited and inciting an all-out war."

"I dinna think so," said Nudd. "That sorta politicking isn'a really goblin style."

The queen rolled her eyes. "Won't commit to a side. Won't broker peace. How exactly do you expect your horde to *turn the tides*? By standing back and watching the flood?"

"Doin' an important thing doesn'a always mean bendin' a whole forest ta yer will," Nudd said. "We canna all be Witchies o' the Wood. Sometimes a small thing just needs a small nudge at exactly the right time. That's what goblins keeps our weathered eyes out fer: the small things ta nudge. And the right times ta nudge 'em."

Before the queen could respond, a shrieking blue blur streaked through the forest and into the pixie ring, collapsing in the pile of mushrooms. A bedraggled blue pixie with wings like a dragonfly and flour in her hair panted and squeaked at her compatriots. The swarm fell silent as they listened to her chitter.

"I'm not fluent in pixie," the queen said quietly, "but that does *not* sound good."

"Dialects is tricky," Nudd whispered to the queen, "but I can tell they're chirpin' about *humans* and about *traps* and about . . . I'm fair sure that last word was *revenge*."

The queen winced.

The air was suddenly hot as the whole colony began to buzz. Blue appeared to have concluded her report, and the hive was breaking into a flurry of furious discussion. Instinctively, the queen glanced up at the spriggan sentinel.

The sober watchman had become not one but a dozen spriggans now, all following the developments silently from the branch. Glistening, beady eyes narrowed as they took in the news unfolding below them. *Oh, perfect*, thought the queen. The whole forest seemed to have become a coiled spring.

The pixies rose into the air as a single entity, the swarm humming with wrathful energy.

"No, no, no. Stay calm." The queen held out her hands,

but the pixies burst past her like azure arrows launching from an invisible bowstring. "Stop!" she commanded.

The pixies did not spare her a backward glance.

"This," said the queen, "is going to end badly."

The branch above them shook, and when the queen glanced up, the spriggans were gone, too.

"This is going to end *very* badly," said Nudd.

"I have a feeling that pixie might have been your *small thing*," the queen mused darkly. "And if you were waiting for your chance to nudge the Wild Wood away from a war—your *right time* may have just passed."

The scruffy bogle watched the cloud of pixies vanish into the woods before turning back to the queen. "I takes the mushrooms now?"

The queen's eye twitched. "Have them." And without another word, she took off after the pixies as quickly as her legs could carry her, Chief Nudd close at her heels.

TWENTY-TWO

ENDSBOROUGH SIMMERED. THE STREETS WERE still crowded, but the tension in the air had shifted from a purposeful rush to a restless discontent. Townsfolk paced the sidewalks or leaned against buildings, gossiping and shaking their heads. Several people had charcoal-black smudges up and down their arms.

"Boys!"

Annie heaved a sigh of relief as her twins jogged across the street to meet her. Soot streaked her face, and her dress was damp at the hip and ash gray at the hem. "The fire is finally out. They had to refill the pumper twice before it was fully doused. Fable! Are you all right?"

"I'm fine," said Fable, catching up to the boys. "I think your town is kinda broken, though."

"Can't argue with that. Oh, your dress is an absolute mess. But I suppose mine isn't much better at the moment."

"Yeah." Fable looked down at herself. "Washing things is not as much fun as getting them dirty."

"And mark my words, ladies and gentlemen!" a voice was booming from the town square. "It will only get worse unless we take a stand! It will only get worse!"

A crowd was gradually coalescing around the center of the grass, where Jacob Hill was orating like a preacher.

"What is he going on about now?" Annie mumbled, and they moved closer to listen in.

"These creatures constitute a public menace!" Hill continued. He stood in front of the same bench where he had carried Oliver Warner after the accident. "A threat to your homes, your families, your children. Now, I've come to know a lot of you personally over the past several weeks. I know Endsborough is full of good, salt-of-the-earth folks. But frankly, I am shocked you've let this go on for so long! Shocked!"

"Hold on just a minute," Mr. Zervos called from the back of the crowd. "I've lived here my whole life, and we've never seen anything like *this* before."

"Haven't you, though?" Hill mused aloud. "How many

of you have had an *experience*?" He passed his eyes over the crowd. "Strange occurrences? Bumps in the night?"

Heads began to nod and meaningful glances were exchanged.

"When I stand on my back porch I can see some kind of lights floating around the garden," someone said. "They show up around sundown, every night, like they're watchin' us."

"Sometimes I find things all moved about in my kitchen in the morning," said someone else. "Feel like I'm going crazy."

"Something took a piece out of my dog's ear," yet another voice cried. "Poor thing growls at the tree line to this day."

"Everyone knows you can't trust them!" said another.

Them. Fable's heart was starting to beat hard against her ribs. *She* was a *them.*

"They've taken people," Old Jim Warner declared loudly. The whispers in the crowd quieted. His eyes turned to Cole and Tinn. "They've *stolen* people."

Fable could see Tinn shrink under Jim's gaze. If Kull had not botched the changeling ritual thirteen years ago, that's exactly what would have happened to the Burtons— Cole would have been stolen away and sold to the fairies, and Tinn would have returned to the Wild Wood to be

211

raised by goblins like he was supposed to be. Old Jim might have gotten used to seeing the twins around town, but he never let them forget that there should only have been one of them. Tinn's obvious discomfort made Fable bristle with anger.

"It's true," Helen Grouse blurted. "Tell him about Joseph, Annie!"

"I don't want to talk about Joseph," Annie said.

"People kept trying to say Annie's husband ran away because of the boys," Helen persisted.

Cole gritted his teeth.

"But she always insisted he would never, didn't you, Annie?" Eyes moved from Mrs. Grouse to Annie. "Those things tried to steal your baby, and when they couldn't take him, they stole your husband instead!"

"Helen, stop." Annie's face was pained.

"Is it true?" Jacob Hill leaned in, his voice softening. "I'm sure you knew your dear husband better than anyone, ma'am. Tell us. Do you believe he *left* you?" He raised his eyebrows. "Or was he *taken*?"

Cole's fingers clenched around the slim disc in his pocket, feeling the coolness of the stone and the etching on its surface. He reached up with his other hand and held his mother's arm. Annie closed her eyes. "Joseph would never leave us," she said.

"*Stolen!*" Hill raised his hands at the confirmation. "And they made you swallow a lie about your sweet husband running away rather than deal with the truth. Yes, I'm beginning to see the pattern here. I'm so sorry, my dear. You deserved better. You all deserve better!"

Hill stepped up onto the bench and addressed the whole group now filling the town square. "It doesn't have to be this way, ladies and gentlemen! For generations you've allowed the creatures of this forest to terrorize you, but if we work together, we can send every last one of the wretched things scurrying for the hills!"

Fable's whole face was hot. "They were already *in* the hills," she growled.

"Fable, don't—" Annie said.

"But it's true!" she yelled. She turned to face Hill directly. "They were *in* the hills that *you* drilled into when this all started. *You're* the one who made the forest mad. Maybe the monsters are just showing you what happens when you cross their line!"

"That!" Hill jabbed a finger at the girl. "That right there! See? That is precisely the attitude they have come to expect from you! How long have you blamed one another for daring to wake the dragon rather than facing the dragon together? My dear, sweet child, human beings do not need *permission* from beasts to tame the land around

213

us! It is *our* world, my friends, not theirs—or it can be, if you've got the mettle. You will never be free from this tyranny unless you make them see what happens when *they* cross *your* line!"

Heads nodded in grim agreement.

"What happens?" a voice from the crowd asked, timidly.

Hill's zealous expression clouded. "What?"

"*What* happens when they cross our line? What exactly are we going to do?"

There was a pause. "You tell me," said Mr. Hill.

Old Jim stepped up to the front of the crowd. "We take a stand," he said. "Hill's right. My nephew is laid up with a broken leg. Our city is on fire. It's time. I think you'll find we've got the mettle, Mr. Hill. And you've got our attention—so what do you propose to do with it?"

Hill lifted his head. "Hm." He surveyed the faces around him. A hundred sets of eyes peered up at him across the crowded square. "Are you all ready," he said, "to stand up for yourselves?"

"Yes!" came a staggered chorus of shouts.

"Are you ready to take back your homes?" he called.

"Yes! Yes!" The voices grew louder.

"Are you ready"—a glint sparkled in Hill's eyes as he gazed around the assembly—"to slay some monsters?"

The blood drained from Fable's face. She sank back against Annie Burton as the energy around her built feverishly. *No,* she thought. *No, no, no.*

"Yes!" the crowd bellowed. "Yes! Yes! Yes!"

"Rally your neighbors," Hill instructed. "Fetch every weapon you can muster. Axes and saws, too. We'll march together to the Roberson Hills and make our stand where they crossed the line! Let's send them a message they won't soon forget!"

The whole world was spinning. Fable couldn't breathe.

"We will make this land ours again, ladies and gentlemen, once and for all," Hill crowed as the crowd began to move out like a pot boiling over. "Even if we have to level the whole miserable forest to do it!"

TWENTY-THREE

B<small>LUE</small> <small>LED</small> <small>THE</small> <small>SWARM.</small> <small>HER</small> <small>NAME</small> <small>WAS</small> <small>NOT</small> *Blue*, of course, but there is no translation in any human language for the customary pixie title that her kinfolk had given her. She had been raised to be wary, to distrust humankind and to shun their gifts. Blue knew better.

But still, the honeyed milk had smelled so sweet. She had allowed it to draw her out of the safety of the trees. Now that was proper tribute, she had thought. It was laid out in a saucer just her size, a ring of flower petals around it, just like in the old days. She had fluttered over cautiously, her eyes fixed on the offering. She had not noticed the human. Or the net.

The glass prison had come next, and then the human building full of horrible human implements. That had been offense enough. She had thought, perhaps, they had seen the error of their ways when they slid in the second offering—an apology, surely. She did not imagine that they would be so cruel as to imprison her twice. But then the metal bars had snapped shut, and Blue had been hauled into the air and shaken mercilessly. The whole ordeal had been beyond an injustice.

If that forest girl had not freed her, surely the humans would have torn her limb from limb or eaten her wings or plucked off her toes one by one. The tales of barbaric human cruelty were legendary. This affront could not go unanswered.

The problem was, now that the town was drawing closer, Blue still did not have any specific answers in mind. Revenge was all well and good—but how? In the old days they had tormented the sheep or tied an offender's hair in miserable knots as they slept. But the men who had harassed her possessed neither sheep nor hair enough to knot. And besides, it felt unequal to their crimes. They deserved far worse punishment.

The swarm slowed as the buildings rose up before them. They were at the forest's edge now. The time for bold actions had arrived. She hesitated, her mind whirring.

And then Blue became aware that the swarm was not alone. Spriggans appeared in the branches and leapt from stump to stone below her. A slate gray spriggan with a face like broken flint called out a formal pixie greeting. His accent was excellent.

Blue nodded to the flinty soldier. The spriggan's eyes looked sharp enough to cut glass. "*We are with you,*" he said in Pixie. "*And with us is the whole of the Wild Wood.*"

Blue looked from her swarm back to the spriggan. "*We wish,*" she stammered, "*to do harm to humans.*"

Flinty smiled coldly. "*Some wishes can be granted.*"

"*You will help us?*"

A nod.

Blue bowed her head. "*What can our humble ring offer your colony to help make the humans pay for a grave injustice?*"

"*You have already given us the only thing we need,*" Flinty crooned. His eyes flashed silver in the light that filtered down through the leaves.

Blue's heart beat fast against her chest. "*What have we given you?*" she asked.

"*A reason,*" he said.

"Mr. Hill, you must end this madness," Annie called, keeping pace with the mob as they plowed forward up the

218

serpentine road. The hum and buzz of the forest around them was growing louder with every step.

"I fully intend to, madam," Hill replied. He pressed forward, using his iron rod like a walking stick. "It's high time somebody did."

Annie shook her head, turning to her neighbors as they soldiered past. "Helen, stop. Amos, this isn't the way! Jim, you're going to get people killed."

"*Doing nothing* is going to get people killed," Old Jim said gruffly, shouldering his rifle. His resolve softened for a fraction of a moment as he caught her eyes. "He was a good man, Annie. Didn't deserve to get took."

"Don't you dare make this absurd crusade about my family," Annie hissed.

Jim shook his head and turned back to the road. "Stand with us or stand aside."

Evie hurried up the road after her great uncle. "Uncle Jim, wait!" she called.

"No. Go back home and tend to your daddy like I told you."

"But—"

"*Now,* Evelyn!"

Evie shuffled to a halt on the side of the road, looking utterly lost. Tinn and Cole gave up their own efforts and joined her.

"They aren't listening," Fable growled. "I think these are the bad men my mama taught me about."

"They're not bad," Evie said, miserably. "They're just . . . scared."

"If they're not scared, they should be," said Tinn. "Things are going to get scary real fast if they start attacking the forest."

The kids watched wretchedly as a parade of townspeople marched past.

Fable shook her head. "I need to warn them."

"Warn who?" said Tinn.

"*Them*," said Fable. "*My* them, the oddlings and the forest folk. They need to run before the humans show up with their axes and their guns."

"And what if they *don't* run?" said Tinn.

"I don't know!" Fable moaned. "I don't know what I'm doing—I never know what I'm doing! But I have to do *something*!" And with that she spun away from the road and began to wade into the bracken.

"Wait!" yelled Cole.

Fable paused. She looked like she wanted to cry. "I have to go," she said. "Mama was right. I should never have come here. Those are *not* my people."

"But *we* are," said Cole.

Fable glanced up. Her eyes were heavy with shadows.

"We're coming with you." Cole looked imploringly at Tinn and Evie. "Right?" They both nodded.

"We're in this together," said Tinn.

"This isn't your forest." Fable shook her head. "The oddlings aren't your people. None of this is your responsibility. Just go home."

"Of course it isn't our forest," said Evie, crossing over the tall grass that lined the road. "But it's *your* forest. And we're your friends. Like it or not, we're not letting you deal with this alone."

Fable managed a weak smile. "You would make a fierce princess," she told Evie. "Predator for sure."

"Let's go," said Tinn. He and Cole bounded into the underbrush together. "And this time how about we *don't* split up?"

The queen ran, the forest flowing past her with every step. She did not vault over troublesome rocks or duck awkwardly under branches. It had been many years since she had found the need to do anything like that. The forest moved for her—with her. They had come to know each other like limbs on the same body. If she ever stumbled, the forest would catch her on instinct, and if the forest ever needed her, she would be its hands. At least, that was how it used to be.

She had long since lost sight of the glimmering pixies, but she trusted the pull of the Wild Wood to guide her. She could no longer hear Chief Nudd or his scouts scrabbling along in her wake, but they would not be far behind. Goblins were nothing if not resourceful.

There were other movements in the underbrush. The queen could feel creatures all around her. Now and then she caught a flutter of wings or a furry flank sliding between the bushes. The forest was always teeming with wildlife—but not like this. The whole forest hummed with an electric energy, like the air before a lightning strike.

She was not far from the human village when she drew to a halt. Muffled voices echoed through the trees ahead. She tensed.

"If Mr. Hill wants to find a monster, he should look in a mirror," grumbled a familiar voice. "At least the monsters in the forest don't spend all their time pretending to be nice and then suddenly turn out to be horrible."

It was Fable. The queen's heart ached. The last time they had spoken, she had told her daughter that she had no friends. She winced at the memory. Of course, Fable was with them now.

"What about kelpies?" asked another voice. One of the twins.

"Well. I mean, sure. There's kelpies," conceded Fable. "Pretending to be nice and then being horrible is basically all kelpies do, yeah. But that's why nobody likes kelpies."

The queen suppressed a smile. Her daughter had listened to a lesson or two after all. She veered toward the voices.

"And changelings?" sighed another voice. "Pretending to be human so my kind could steal babies is apparently what I was born for." That would be Tinn.

The queen kept herself to the shadows as she neared. She peered around a tree trunk. Fable was a dozen paces away, accompanied by both twins and the girl from the village—Evie. They crossed a fallen log together.

"Well, true," Fable admitted. "But you're no good at being horrible. And my mama says Chief Nudd put a stop to all that, anyway. Mama wouldn't be friends with goblins if they were bad. She always does what's right for the forest. She's a good Witch of the Wood."

The queen felt a lump in her throat and her chest tightened. Her daughter thought she was a good witch.

"The point is," Fable added, "Mr. Hill is a butt."

"He's actually been really nice—especially after the accident," Evie said. "He helped my dad get settled in at home and he paid for all his doctor bills. He's come by every day to check up on him and bring him soup and other stuff to make him feel better. He even stuck around to keep me company while Dad was resting. He says my drawings are really good. Today, though—he's like a whole different person."

"He isn't even supposed to be here anymore," Cole said. "After the giant, he said he was done trying to find oil and was going to go back to selling tonics in the city. I wish he had."

"I don't think he's actually bad on the inside," Evie said. "His tonic really works, did you know? He gave my dad this 'fortifying elixir' he made himself. He calls it his golden goose. Said it was supposed to boost Dad's strength, and it did! Yesterday my dad even felt good enough to try walking a few steps. Mr. Hill was really proud of him."

"That's great and everything," said Fable, "but a spoonful of medicine isn't gonna protect all the innocent forest folk about to get killed."

The queen straightened.

"NOT KILL FOREST FOLK!" thundered a voice like a wet avalanche.

The queen froze. Ice ran through her veins as a nearby boulder unfolded itself with a grinding noise and a spray of dirt and dry moss.

"FOREST FOLK KILL YOU!"

TWENTY-FOUR

As one, the children skidded to a stop.

In front of them loomed a figure made of living rock. The brute was nine feet tall and almost as wide across from shoulder to shoulder. Stony fists clenched and unclenched with a grinding crunch. Each one of the creature's massive hands looked as if it probably weighed as much as all four children combined. The troll's eyes glowed a soft orange within their granite sockets.

"HUMANS BAD!" Stony muscles flexed with a sound like shifting bricks as the granite goliath stomped forward. Cole stood frozen directly in its path. "HUMANS WANT KILL FOREST FOLK."

"Th-that's a rock troll!" Evie stammered. "I have a whole page about them."

"Hey!" Cole yelled. "We're not trying to kill anybody!"

The troll raised its fists over its head—but before it could bring them down on Cole's skull, a hillside of fur and muscles erupted from behind a nearby tree and slammed into the boy, rolling with him out of the way of the rocky fists. The troll's blow left a deep divot in the soft earth, and sent leaves spinning down the forest floor.

A few feet away, the furry shape unfurled to deposit Cole back on his feet again, confused but unharmed. He looked up to find himself face-to-face with a grizzly. The bear huffed and Cole's hair fluttered.

"Mama?" Fable said. The bear-queen met her gaze.

"SMALL ONES WARNED TROLLKIN ABOUT HUMANS," the troll growled, taking a second wide swing, this time for Fable. She dodged narrowly out of his reach. "HUMANS BAD! HOLD STILL, HUMANS! BE DEAD!"

In one fluid motion, the bear stood up on her hind legs, threw back her head, and spun, her thick hide becoming a cloak once more. The queen stood before the troll, her face a mask of royal fury. "Nobody is killing anybody!" she declared.

"HUMAN NOT TELL TROLL WHAT TO DO." The brute's glowing orange eyes focused on the queen. "NO MORE."

The queen held her ground, locked in a battle of wills as she faced down the troll—but Fable could see that the creature was unmoved. If anything, his stony expression only grew angrier.

"Wait!" Fable yelled. She threw herself forward between her mother and the troll just as it raised its fists again. The troll did not wait.

The troll swung. Fable threw her hands in front of her face, a futile defense from the mountain of rock descending toward her.

"No!" the queen cried.

And then the universe hiccuped.

There was a *crack*, like the snapping of a thick rubber band, and then a whoosh of air, as though someone had opened a door in the middle of a storm. Fable's insides felt like soap bubbles in a whirlwind and she fought back a tingling pressure inside her head.

The queen gasped. One instant, bulging rocky knuckles had been driving toward her daughter like a runaway freight train—and the next, the two of them were being showered in a deluge of tiny, glossy pebbles instead.

Fable blinked dust out of her eyes. The troll was gone. Slowly, she lowered her arms. Her legs felt wobbly and she was dizzy. She shook her head as the tingling ebbed.

A bulging hill of pebbles, smooth as river rocks, stood before her, tinkling quietly over her toes as it settled. The pile shifted, and the queen and all four children stared as a drab green dome rose to the surface. Gradually, a wobbling tortoise emerged from the pile. It had knobbly legs that moved uncertainly as it pulled itself through the heap of stones. It turned a pair of orange eyes accusingly toward Fable.

"Is that . . . ?" Tinn let the question hang in the air.

"Did you . . . ?" Cole began.

"You just turtled that troll!" Evie finished. "That's so awesome!"

Fable looked sheepishly at her mother. "I didn't mean to."

The queen had to remind herself to breathe again. Master-level mages in the Annwyn could not have pulled off a transfiguration like that—not with years to study and prepare.

"Are you going to say something?" said Fable.

The queen straightened. She glanced at the children. "You should not have brought them here," she said.

Fable swallowed. "I went to the people village," she

said. "I know I wasn't supposed to. But I did—I had to. It's bad, Mama, and it's about to get a lot worse."

The queen shook her head. "Their world is *not* our world, Fable."

"It *was* your world, though," Fable said. "Before the goblins took you away from it. It could be your world again. It was *grandma's* world, too."

The queen bristled. "Endsborough turned their backs on your grandmother," she hissed. "The world of men is monstrous, child. They drove her away when she needed them most, and she denounced them in return. I will not discuss this any—"

"But they *didn't*," Fable said. "Not all of them. While you were gone, some of them were awful, sure, but some of them made up songs for grandma when she was all alone, and they sang them at the forest's edge to cheer her up."

The queen hesitated. "You don't know what you're talking about, Fable."

"I do. I met somebody who remembers her. You should meet her, too. Grandma didn't turn her back on people. Not all of them, anyway. She left them gifts. She believed in them. There are places where the forest meets the town. What if *that's* our world?"

The queen stared at Fable, and a million melancholy thoughts played across the woman's eyes.

"I need you to remember that," Fable added nervously, "when I tell you about the other thing."

The queen listened in horror as Fable recounted the rapidly unfolding situation. The whole of the Wild Wood bristled as she finished.

"And the humans are on their way?" The queen looked pale. "*Now?*"

Fable nodded. "They're planning on making their stand where it all started. That's why we need to get there first. We need to warn the whole forest."

Hooves pounded across the earth behind them. Beyond the bushes, a snow-white stag leapt through the trees. Lights whipped along in the branches behind it, and all around sounded the grunts and growls of countless unseen beasts joining the race in a steady current, descending on the northwest corner of the Wild Wood. A pair of beady eyes glinted in the foliage, and for a brief second the queen caught sight of a flinty spriggan looking down on them, his mouth cracked upward in a wry grimace. A moment later he, too, had vanished into the woods.

"I think," said the queen numbly, "that maybe the forest already knows."

"What are we going to do?" asked Fable.

"*You* are going to take these three back to their homes." The queen took a deep breath. "And under no circumstances are you to go anywhere near that Grandmother Tree. I *forbid* it, Fable."

Before Fable could even open her mouth to protest, her mother was gone.

The children stood in stunned silence for several seconds.

"What happens now?" said Evie at last.

Tinn and Cole looked at Fable.

"She *forbade* us from going to the Grandmother Tree," said Fable. She took a deep breath. "But there is no Grandmother Tree out there. Not anymore." She looked at her friends. "Of course we're going."

TWENTY-FIVE

THE QUEEN'S LUNGS BURNED AS SHE BURST OUT
of the trees and into the open field. She tried to breathe
evenly. This was no time to show weakness.

The clearing bristled. Oddlings and fair folk of all sorts
peered up from the tall grasses: lumbering trollkin, shifty
gnomes, and solemn spirits. Skoll, the fiercest wolf of the
Warg, had come from his den in the far south, flanked by
the strongest of his pack. Pholon, high general of the centaur herd, stood with a spear in his hands. Even Lutin, a
usually cheerful hob, had draped himself in a chain mail
vest and leaned on a knotted cudgel in place of his customary cane. Hundreds of creatures crowded around the

edge of the ruined field in a motley crescent, and hundreds more shook the nearby branches and rustled the ferns just inside the cover of the forest. This assembly had converged for a single purpose.

"You would enter into battle without informing your queen?" The queen kept her voice steady and even, but she wondered if the more perceptive beasties around her could hear her heart pounding.

A chittering, scratchy voice cut through the noise. *"The queen knows all that happens in her forest, does she not?"* it asked in Spriggan. A figure with a face like a broken flint emerged from the grasses and swung itself gracefully up onto a tree stump. *"Does the all-knowing queen now need to be* informed?"

The queen pursed her lips.

"A queen of almosts," Flinty said in sardonic English, eyes fixed on hers, but his chattering words loud enough for the whole assembly to hear. "Almost fairy. Almost human. Now it is almost time. Does she know what she is, in the end?"

"You dare?" the queen growled through gritted teeth.

"The humans are coming," Flinty said. "Time to make choices. Will you stand with us? Or with them?"

Fable, Evie, and the boys raced through the forest. Now and then a fairy buzzed past their heads, and vibrant yellow eyes shot them glances through the leaves.

"I've never seen this many creatures in one place at a time," Tinn whispered. He slid across a wide tree trunk that spanned a babbling stream. They had almost reached the Roberson Hills.

"I could fill a hundred journals with all this," Evie said, hopping down after him.

"We're almost there," said Fable. "It's just over this ridge." She scrambled up a mossy embankment. "The field should be just—oh. Oh dang." She stood up, eyes wide.

Trolls and pixies and enormous wolves filled the field ahead. A beast with a horse's body and the torso of a man clutched a long spear beside a woman whose lower half melted into the iridescent scales of an enormous snake's tail. Fable knew the centaur and naga clans were anything but allies, and yet here they stood, side by side, united against a common enemy. Beasts and beings continued to spill out of the trees, the ranks of their wild army swelling.

"I don't think the forest needs protecting," Tinn breathed. His face paled. "If the townspeople walk into this, they'll be massacred."

A single figure detached herself from the group and stepped into the center of the clearing. Her bearskin cloak swept the dusty ground. Hundreds of glinting eyes followed the Queen of the Deep Dark.

A series of harsh, hissing clicks followed. Fable held her breath as her mother turned to face a feral crowd.

"I stand," the queen declared loudly and clearly, "with the forest."

And then the first shot rang out.

TWENTY-SIX

Crouching at the edge of the clearing, the children watched as the puff of smoke lifted into the wind. It wasn't a loud boom. It was hardly even a bang. The gunshot that cracked the air was no louder than a thick branch snapping off a tree. For one slow, breathless moment, silence followed—a sizzling quiet, like a burning fuse.

Albert Townshend had been the first to pull the trigger. He was a quiet young man only a handful of years older than Tinn and Cole. Albert collected bottle caps and washed dishes at the Lucky Pig. He had never aimed that heavy pistol at a living thing before. Truth be told, he

236

hadn't properly aimed it this time—he had merely lifted the muzzle in the general direction of the unholy horde and squeezed. His hand was still shaking after the smoke had drifted away.

The shot hummed over the pointy hats of the gnomes and sang over the naga's scaly shoulder until it buried itself in the rough hide of Skoll, fiercest wolf of the Warg. Albert did not know that Skoll was the fiercest wolf of the Warg, just as Skoll did not know that Albert was the most average dishwasher in the Lucky Pig on Tuesdays through Saturdays. What they both knew—what every anxious observer around that silent clearing knew immediately—was that Albert Townshend had made a terrible mistake.

The great wolf flinched as if stung. He glanced down at his flank and then up the sloping hill at the shaking Albert. His lips curled back over razor-sharp fangs. Muscles rippled under layers of coarse hair. Skoll growled, a noise so low it was barely a noise anymore.

"This is going to be bad," Tinn muttered, just before the field erupted into complete chaos.

Skoll made straight for Albert, but he was not as fast as the arrow that caught the dishwasher in the shoulder and sent him falling over backward with a yelp. More shots were fired, cracking and popping in irregular bursts. Sunlight flashed off of wicked blades, and deafening cries of pain and outrage filled the air, along with clouds of acrid gun smoke and buzzing, flapping wings.

"Ow!" Mr. Washington shrieked as a blur of wings swarmed around him. "Ow! They're biting!" His flailing arms made contact and a stunned pixie spun to the ground with a squeak.

In all the madness, Fable had lost sight of her mother. She squinted through the scuffle and the smoke, her eyes searching. A flinty-faced spriggan in the center of the bedlam opened the pouch he kept slung around his neck. He tossed his head back and threw something in the back of his throat. Was that little ruffian having a snack in the middle of a battle?

"What do we do?" Cole whispered.

Fable didn't have an answer. More townspeople were pouring down the hillsides now. A woman in a soot-stained apron pulled at her neighbors' arms, but they shoved past her to join the fray.

"Is that Mom?" Tinn breathed. "Oh, jeez, she's right in the middle!"

Even over all the other voices, Annie Burton's fruitless pleas carried on the wind. "Stop! Don't do this!" she implored.

"There's my uncle Jim, too," Evie whispered. "What are they all *doing*? They're going to get killed!"

238

Fable looked where Evie was pointing. Old Jim Warner had paused atop the nearest hill, overlooking the melee. He lifted the rifle and focused his aim on a target the children could not see within the fight. His jaw tightened. For all his mean talk, he did not look enthusiastic about pulling the trigger.

Fable wondered with icy dread which of the forest folk might be standing at the other end of his muzzle. Kallra? Chief Nudd? Her mother?

Old Jim's thumb slid to the hammer, but before he could fire his first shot, the swirling smoke of the battlefield parted and a giant erupted before him like a whale breaching the ocean's surface.

Old Jim stared, gaping.

The impossible behemoth loomed over the heads of even the tallest trolls, its skin like hardened slate and its expression murderous. The monster's features blurred at the edges, and Fable found it hard to focus on the giant for too long. It made her eyes hurt.

Old Jim slowly lowered his rifle. Across the next hill, Annie Burton froze. The colossus was growing larger still, right before her eyes. It was thirty feet tall—then forty— then fifty. The ground shuddered as it stepped forward, and the children could only stare, stupefied. Gunshots rang out to the left and right, but bullets whizzed right through the giant's skin and out the other side as if it weren't even there. The giant took a slow step toward Annie.

"Mom!" Tinn yelled. "Look out!" If she could hear him, she was too stunned to react. Cole felt his heart lurch.

Jim Warner jogged toward Annie. "Move!" he bellowed. Annie blinked. Old Jim caught her by the shoulder and she snapped out of her daze. The two of them leapt just as the giant swung one mammoth hand downward.

Annie dove to one side, Jim to the other. Annie rolled to safety.

Evie screamed as Old Jim's body flew fifty feet in the air to land in a heap in the center of the smoky field. His rifle tumbled across the grass and slid to a stop against the roots of the felled tree.

Tinn's throat felt dry as he swallowed. Old Jim wasn't moving.

Evie vaulted forward.

"No, wait!" Fable tried to catch her arm, but Evie threw herself into the fray. Tinn bolted after her, Cole fast on his heels.

The myriad sounds of battle melted into a deafening roar as the children pelted between slicing blades and slashing claws. Evie ducked under a troll's swinging fist and Cole dodged a swiping spear tip. Fable heard a *pop* and felt the air part in front of her as something shot past, inches from her face. She couldn't seem to catch her breath, and for all her frantic searching, there was no sign of her mother in the crush of bodies.

Somehow, in the fog of smoke and sound, Evie found Old Jim and threw herself down at his side. "He's still breathing!" she cried. "He's alive!"

No sooner had she spoken than an arrow thudded into the soil a foot away from Jim's leg, the bolt vibrating from the force of impact.

"He won't be alive for long if we can't get him somewhere safe," said Tinn.

"Where is safe?" said Cole.

Hoofbeats thudded up behind them like thunder, and in the next instant a pair of centaurs leapt over their heads. The kids threw themselves down, feeling the ground shake as the hooves slammed to the earth and pounded off again into the fog of war. Somewhere behind them a voice bellowed something loud and incoherent. A shrill screech answered.

Fable's head spun. It was all too much. The gun smoke hanging over the field stung her eyes and burned her throat. "Stop," she tried to say, but she couldn't even hear her own voice over the din.

"We can't stay here!" yelled Cole.

"We're not leaving him," said Evie.

"Come on!" Tinn grabbed Old Jim under one arm. "Anywhere is better than here. Let's just find some cover." Cole grabbed Jim's other arm. Jim let out a low moan, his head lolling to one side as they tugged at him.

They dragged the old man toward the wreckage of the ruined oil rig, keeping their heads low as they moved. They had barely reached the shadow of the shattered structure when an unearthly wild pig bounded out of the fog, its eyes like embers and its back lined with spines as jagged and sharp as saw blades. Cole threw himself aside just in time to avoid being cut to ribbons.

Fable raised her eyes and tried to calm her pounding heart. It was too much. Through the haze to the east, she could see spear tips waving. Atop the hill to the west, a group of townspeople had set a hay cart ablaze, and they looked as though they might send it rolling down. All the while, the air crackled with the incessant popping of gunshots.

"Stop!" Fable screamed. "Stop! Stop! Stop!" She was choking on noise and smoke and violence. At the top of the hill, the blazing hay cart began to roll. It caught a rough patch a few yards down and toppled, spewing its fiery contents across the hillside like a hellish blanket.

"We can't stay here!" Cole yelled. "We need to—"

But he did not finish. A booming voice from the forest's edge barked a command and the sky was suddenly full of arrows. The projectiles looked strangely graceful as they reached the top of their arc, moving toward the children like a hungry swarm.

Time stopped.

Fable's heart paused. In that frozen moment, the strangling panic lifted, the deafening noise died away, and she felt herself go hollow and empty.

Thum. Her heart beat. *Thum.* The pounding echoed through her, rippling the tips of her fingers. *Thum.* Magic tingled in Fable's veins.

Fable's mind was clear and calm. Cole was shouting something, but his voice was a million miles away. Evie had thrown herself over her great uncle's chest, and Tinn had thrown himself over Evie.

Fable took a deep breath.

And then she let it out through the wind.

The breeze moved through Fable and Fable moved through the breeze. *Gale,* she thought. Trees whistled, smoke whorled, and with a *whoosh*, the swarm of descending arrows curved abruptly upward, their sharp tips sweeping over the children's heads to bury themselves harmlessly in the burning hillside. The flames crackled happily and began to consume the shafts at once.

Fable closed her eyes. She felt the heat of the raging fire, and reached out for it in her mind and grasped it with a hand that could not be burned. *Extinguish.* Her fingers clenched at her sides as she concentrated. She felt the flames cool by slow degrees under the pressure of her mental grip, until they were no warmer than a summer breeze—and when she opened her eyes, the fire was out. A cloud of ash and smoke spun lazily over the charred earth.

Fable turned back to Cole and Tinn and Evie, still huddled over Old Jim, their arms around each other in the shadow of the broken rig. Cole's urgent shouts reached Fable like a gentle whisper. He was yelling at her to get down, and Tinn was waving for her frantically. Their eyes were full of fear but also desperate hope. Fable smiled. Her friends wanted to protect her.

She listened. She breathed. She concentrated.

She wanted to protect them, too.

And so she did.

TWENTY-SEVEN

THE BREEZE SHIFTED, AND THE QUEEN'S CLOAK whipped in the draft. She felt a familiar tingle running up her neck, but she kept her focus. There were six of them, men and boys, racing across the gap toward the waiting gnome forces. The human fools wielded kitchen knives and broken table legs. Perhaps they thought their height would give them the advantage. They would not survive the encounter. The gnomes tensed as they waited for the men to close the final distance.

The queen flexed. At her command, the grass slithered with motion and the first man tumbled to the ground. Not remotely enough time to summon a full wall, but she could fill the field with knotty, troublesome roots. The second man twisted as he stumbled and she could hear the snap of his ankle. He howled in pain. Better a broken ankle than his life lost. The rest of the men slowed, stepping more gingerly through the growing tangle, the momentum of their terrible decision rapidly losing steam.

Goose bumps prickled across the queen's arms, and she felt it again, stronger this time. She knew that magic. So much energy was swirling in the air all around her—fairies and spirits and wildlings of all sorts wielding their own spells and charms—but this magic was special. Where was it coming from? It was like trying to pick out a familiar voice in a chorus. And there it was.

Fable's magic.

No. Her daughter could not be here. Not now.

The queen took two steps forward, and then, halfway across the field, a circle of earth rose like a platform. Roots pushed up out of the ground and spun themselves into thick vines, which wove into tighter and tighter knots, fat leaves sprouting from their sides in rippling emerald waves. It was a nature barrier—a wild-wall as sturdy and thick as any the queen had ever summoned. It grew with lightning speed, weaving a circular barrier twenty feet in diameter. In its center—through the fog, and between the rapidly closing gaps in the vines—the queen could see a head of dark, curly hair.

"Fable," she breathed.

Within the wild-wall, Fable took a slow breath. She could still hear the pop of gunfire and the clang of steel—but inside their leafy cocoon the noises were muffled and far away.

Cole stood and brushed his hands off on his pants. "Whoa," he said. "Nice."

Fable blinked and spun, surveying the wall with unmasked wonder. "Huh. Yeah. I—I did this." She nodded to herself. "This is a thing I did. Now what?"

The ground within the circle was cracked and uneven, churned up by the motion of the roots. The framework of the fractured rig was now leaning even more heavily to one side. Beside it, a wicked-looking tricone drill bit had been partially unearthed, its muddy teeth glistening in the sunlight.

Tinn pushed himself to his feet. "Old Jim is still breathing, but he's in bad shape." He leaned his back against the ruins of the rig, and the wreck creaked and groaned. He pulled hastily away as it swayed ominously.

"I guess now we know Hill was telling the truth about what smashed that thing," Cole said. "That was a real, actual giant back there. Old Jim is lucky it didn't just crush him completely. I thought there were no giants left in the Wild Wood."

"There aren't," said Fable. "Not . . . technically."

"How was that *not* a giant?"

"I'm pretty sure it was a spriggan. But a big one."

"I thought spriggans were tiny," said Evie.

"They are," Fable said. "Except when they're not. They're forest spirits. And spirits are . . . flexible. Some of them turn into plants, or winter winds, or bullfrogs. Some of them turn into . . . well, *that*, apparently. They can't stay giant forever, though. So, that was a temporary giant. Doesn't count."

"Spirits of the old giants," Tinn mumbled, more to himself than the rest of the group, remembering Kull's lesson.

Fable nodded. "That's right. Mama once told me that spriggans could make themselves huge if they needed to— I'd forgotten all about that until I saw it. I've never ever actually seen one do it. It basically never happens."

"They probably haven't had a reason to for a long time," said Cole. "Not with the old saw mill closed down and people not chopping down trees anymore—plus your mom protecting the forest for them."

"Well, they have reason now," Fable said. "Humans ruin everything."

Nobody said anything for several moments as the dull roar of the battle continued all around them.

"Hey. Look at this," said Evie, breaking the silence. "There's stuff all over the bottom of the drill."

They turned to look where she was pointing. The drill was a heavy industrial thing, built for tunneling through rock. It ended in a trio of jagged cones all rimmed with metal teeth—and each of these was caked in some sort of iridescent mud. It glittered like diamonds where it caught the light.

"Is that oil?" said Tinn.

"It doesn't look like any kind of oil I've ever seen," said Evie. She stepped closer. "It looks like clay, but there's all these sparkles in it, like it's full of tiny rainbows." Light bouncing off of the drill cast a spray of colors across Evie's arms like fancy confetti as she neared. She poked at the mud and a clump broke off in her hand. "It's all powdery," she said, dropping the lump to the ground.

A shadow fell over the circle of vines, and all four children looked up. A massive face like sheets of granite stared down at them. It did not look happy.

"Your temporary giant," Cole managed in a hoarse whisper, "appears to be still a giant."

The giant's fingers ground slowly closed to form a fist the size of a boulder.

"Look out!" yelled Tinn.

"Stay away from my friends!" Fable cried. She pointed both hands at the giant and screwed up her eyes in concentration. Nothing happened. She opened her eyes. "Oh, come *on*," she growled. "Stupid magic! You're supposed to *work* now!"

The giant's fist rose to strike.

Fable pointed both hands upward again. "Be a hedgehog!" she yelled. "Butterfly? Turtle?" The giant—still very much a giant—drove his fist down like an avalanche.

Evie dove, catching Fable from the side a split second before the stony knuckles could catch her from above. The two tumbled over the uneven terrain, bouncing as the impact of the giant's blow shook the earth. Something behind them cracked loudly, and they could hear the boys yelp in alarm. Evie's face ground against the dirt and Fable flopped beside her. They righted themselves frantically as the giant's fist withdrew, bracing for the next attack. But the behemoth turned away. It bellowed deeply as its attention was drawn elsewhere.

"You okay?" Fable panted.

Evie did a rapid inventory of limbs and nodded, wiping dust out of her eyes. Everything hurt and she could taste iron on her tongue. With one hand she wiped a bloody lip, and with the other she pushed herself to her feet. She swayed.

"I'm . . ." she began. Her whole head suddenly buzzed and her knees felt wobbly. It took everything she had left not to topple over. Then, just as quickly, the sensation was gone. ". . . I'm fine?"

Evie took a deep breath and was shocked to feel her lungs expand without pain—she hadn't even realized how sore they had become until they weren't. Had Fable done something magical to her? Her joints, which had been screaming at her since they had begun their reckless race through the forest, felt strangely limber and strong. She looked down at her hand. Across her fingers was a streak of red from her bloody lip—and within the smear sparkled the residue of the glittering powder. Evie blinked, trying to make sense of the feelings coursing through her.

"Help!" Tinn's voice sounded strained, and Evie pulled her attention toward it. "Help me!" he cried. "I can't move it!"

What remained of the rig had collapsed completely. The giant's blow must have finished it off. Steel braces had bent and twisted, and splintered scraps of wood littered the ground to the left and right of Old Jim. Extraordinarily, the man seemed to have missed the worst of it, but Tinn had not been so lucky.

A timber as thick across as Tinn's chest had landed on the boy's leg. Tinn's face was pale. Cole was already at his brother's side, and in an instant Fable had bounded over to join them. They pulled as Tinn pushed, their arms shaking from the strain, but the heavy beam refused to budge.

Evie ran forward and wedged her fingers under the wood beside them. Maybe, if they all pulled at the same time . . .

The beam lifted a fraction as her fingers slid under it. Evie tensed. Her muscles tightened. The beam rose.

She almost dropped it the second it was up. She had expected the dead weight of a mountain, but the wood under her fingers felt soft and light, like she was lifting a cardboard box and not a timber as wide as she was. She gripped tighter and raised it over her head, her fingers pressing into the pliant wood like it was a sponge.

Fable took hold of Tinn's arms and dragged him out. It took Evie a moment to realize that Cole had let go of the beam as well. He stood back, gaping at her. She, alone, was holding the heavy beam aloft.

"How?" Cole managed.

The timber thudded like a falling tree as Evie dropped it.

Evie looked from Cole to Fable to Tinn. Tinn was lying flat on his back. He was starting to look green, but she couldn't tell if this was from the pain or if his goblin blood was kicking in under the strain. Finally she looked down at her own hands again. She felt queasy. "I—I don't know," she mumbled.

"Seriously?" said Cole. "So, does *everybody* get to have amazing powers except for me?"

"Nice job," said Fable. "Is magic strength a princess thing?"

Evie's insides were twisting in knots. "What's happening to me?" she said.

"Grind his . . . bones," mumbled Tinn, "to make . . . my bread."

"Is he delirious?" said Cole.

"No—listen." Tinn pushed himself up to sitting with great effort, wincing as the weight on his leg shifted. "Kull told me . . . giants used to have this tradition . . . of eating the bodies of their dead . . . so their essence could live on. They literally ground their bones to make bread."

"That sparkly stuff on the drill," said Cole. "You think that's dead giants?"

"I rubbed my lip," said Evie, blinking. The wooziness was beginning to wear off, but her stomach was still rolling. "I was bleeding."

"I think maybe," Tinn grunted, "you got some giant . . . in your bloodstream."

"I don't feel good," said Evie. "I think I might be sick."

"No wonder they're so angry!" blurted Fable. "It was never about the tree at all! Spriggans aren't *tree* spirits, they're the spirits of *giants*! That's why they protect these parts. It's their burial ground! Holy heck. Are *all* the Grandmother Trees growing on top of dead giants?"

"Hill wasn't just taking soil samples," said Cole. "He was robbing a grave, and he didn't even realize it. *That's* why giants destroyed his pump."

"And why the spriggans have been going around the forest trying to get everyone all jumpy about humans!" Fable clenched her fist. "I *told* Hill this was his fault!"

"I think we just figured out the secret ingredient to Hill's 'fortifying elixir,'" said Evie with a shudder. Her head was clearing, and she once more felt as if she had run a marathon. "Ugh. My dad's been drinking diluted giant corpse for days."

"This is it!" Cole said, his eyes alight. "This is how we stop the fighting!"

Three sets of eyes turned toward him.

"Hill might not have known what he had, but he knew it was special. He saved all the soil samples. He still has them stashed somewhere. His *golden goose*, remember? We just need to get him to return what he stole so the spirits of the giants can be at peace. Peaceful giants, peaceful spriggans, peaceful forest. We can all call off the attack."

"You really think it'll work?" said Tinn.

"I think it's better than waiting for everybody to kill each other," Cole said. "You think you can walk?"

Tinn pushed himself up. His face contorted and he collapsed back to the ground immediately. He shook his head. "I don't think so," he grunted.

"I'll stay with Tinn," said Evie. "Go. You two will be faster without us."

Fable looked at Cole. Cole nodded.

"Okay," Fable said. "All we have to do is find a guy in the middle of a battlefield and convince him to give his golden goose to a bunch of monsters."

"Preferably before anybody murders him," said Cole. "Or us."

"Right," said Fable. "Here goes."

TWENTY-EIGHT

It took three tries, but the wild-wall finally parted in response to Fable's urging. The knots unfurled reluctantly in front of her, unraveling and reshaping until they formed a narrow, arched opening.

"Good luck," said Evie.

"Keep Tinn safe," said Cole.

Evie gave him an earnest nod, and Cole returned it.

"Stay close," Fable said.

"Right behind you," Cole promised.

And then Fable and Cole were through the gap and back into the field of battle. The screams and shouts and snarls hit Fable like a charging bull. The air tasted like spent matches. The smoke had only gotten worse, and it made her eyes water as she and Cole pressed forward. A gun went off so close Fable's ears rang.

Cole put a hand on her shoulder and pointed.

Thirty feet ahead, Jacob Hill stood atop the wide stump of the Grandmother Tree. He held his iron rod in both hands as he peered through the fog.

"Don't let them get around you!" he shouted over his shoulder at the ragtag battalion of farmers, carpenters, and grocery clerks who formed his motley front line. "Hold! Hold there and wait to advance together! We will finish this as one!"

Hill's perch was in the eye of the storm, a no-man's-land between opposing forces. It gave him a view overlooking the melee, but it also made him the clearest target on the field. He swung the rod at a throng of brownies as they buzzed around his head, and the swarm scattered, chittering angrily.

"Mr. Hill!" Cole cried as they neared the stump. "Mr. Hill, we know how to end the fighting!"

"What in blazes?" Hill's eyes widened as he locked on to them. "Get behind the line! You kids are going to get yourselves killed! Hurry!"

"You don't understand," Cole called up to him. "Listen!"

"I said fall back!"

On their right, a troll let out a bellow—something between the roar of a lion and the rumble of a rock slide—and then broke into a run toward the human forces. To the left, the humans answered with a cry of "Attack!" and the whole line charged forward.

"Please!" Fable yelled. "We know how to stop this!"

"You think you can *stop* this?" Hill looked incredulously down at her. "Little girl, you *can't*. Now fall back!"

Fable's fists clenched. "It's no use," Cole said, tugging her arm. "Come on!"

You can't. To the right, more forest factions had joined the charge behind the lumbering troll, and to the left, humans were pouring out of the hills. *You can't.* Great waves of combatants were now closing in on either side of them. *You can't.* Every *you can't* Fable had heard over the past frustrating week echoed back at her. *You can't* have a foot in both worlds. *You can't* attend people school. *You can't* have human friends. *You can't* make the world what you want it to be. *You can't* compel people.

Fable felt the tingling pressure building inside her skull again. "No," she said aloud. The word was quiet but firm, and it cut across the smoky air like a blade. "*Everyone else* can fall back."

The universe, which had been listening in the background like a patient hound, responded to her command without hesitation.

Reality lurched. The charging troll felt it first. Not pain—which was surprising, given his understanding of how war was supposed to feel—but tightness. The sensation wrapped itself around his bones and lifted him off his meaty feet. The naga, nixies, and nymphs all felt it, too, a gentle yet inescapable grip as the universe pulled them backward toward the forest's edge. The centaurs' hooves dug deep grooves in the soil as they were dragged away. On the human side, several fighters dropped their pitchforks and cleavers in alarm as the invisible cords of Fable's will drew townspeople up into the hills.

In a matter of seconds, the battlefield was empty, still, and quiet.

Fable could hear her heartbeat in her ears. She swallowed.

Jacob Hill's eyes were wide as he stared down at her. "You have my attention," he managed.

Silence hung over the empty field and clung like dew to the hillside. The queen felt her feet slide to a halt in the damp pine needles, her eyes still fixed on Fable in the foggy distance. She wanted to race across the desolate field toward her daughter, but her body refused to respond.

"Yer Majesty."

The queen's eyes flicked to her left. In the underbrush beside her, a drab green face peered up at her from beneath a weathered top hat.

"Thief King," she acknowledged drily. "Have you been hiding in the bracken this entire time?"

Chief Nudd gave an unapologetic shrug.

The queen rolled her eyes and turned them back to her daughter. "So glad you're here to help with all those *small things*," she said under her breath.

"Otch. Small things is easy. Anyone can handle a small thing. *Right times* is harder."

"You keep waiting for your right time, then," the queen growled. "The rest of us will have to do what we can with the time we've got."

On the other side of the barren field, Annie Burton swayed as she tried to catch her breath. Even from this distance, she recognized the boy in the middle of the clearing. "Cole?" Her chest ached to run to him. That man on the tree stump—Hill—was saying something to her son, and then Cole's hands gestured frantically as he responded. Annie's muscles strained. Oh, why couldn't she move?

"Now do you understand?" Cole finished.

Fable's mind was still reeling from the magic that had coursed through her. She had felt connected to all of those people, all at once. For just a moment, they were her and she was them, and all of them were one.

Hill's eyes drifted between the two children, warily. "I believe you," he said at last. "But they're not getting my powder."

"What?" said Fable. "But you *just* said you believe us!"

"I do. But do you think I'm a fool? We are in the middle of a war, and you expect me to give my enemy the means to annihilate us? You think I don't know what you're asking me to surrender? You think I don't see you for what you are?"

"For what we are?" said Fable. "We're the ones trying to save lives here!"

"Your own lives," said Hill. "Yours and your kind. I didn't recognize it at first—but after that display of yours, you can't pretend you aren't one of them."

Fable scowled, her jaw set. She was getting very tired of other people telling her which side she was on.

"And you." Hill turned to Cole. "I should have seen it earlier. You're the changeling, I presume? It had to be one of you. Tinn, is it? Where is your so-called brother, now? Or have you finally shown your true colors and done away with him?"

"I'm not—" Cole scowled. "Wait. How do *you* know about me and my brother?"

Hill straightened. "I've learned a lot of things in the past few days. Oh, yes, I know all about Endsborough's goblin boys. And a lot more than that. Ogres. Trolls. Spriggans."

Fable narrowed her eyes. "If you know about spriggans, then you should know that what you took belongs to them. You know you need to give it back. Please. Do the right thing."

"I *am* doing the right thing! Don't try to make me the villain. I'm the good guy, here." Hill opened his jacket and the kids could see eight shiny glass tubes poking out of the inner pocket, each stoppered with a cork. Hill plucked one out and held it in the light. It glistened blindingly, the same iridescent powder as they had seen on the drill, but without any dust or clay to dull its sheen. "Do you have any idea how many people could benefit from this powder? How many lives it could save?"

"If you give those to us, it could save a whole lot of them right now," said Fable.

262

"This? This is hardly a fraction of what I've collected," Hill said. "I'm not dumb enough to bring my entire stock into battle." He turned the tube in his hand, his eyes glittering with bright reflections as it spun. "I was drilling for crude oil, but what I found was so much more valuable. There are people around the world who would pay anything to get their hands on my discovery."

"People are trying to kill each other, and you're thinking about the price?" demanded Cole.

"It isn't about the money." Hill shook his head, pulling his eyes back to the children. "I spent *years* peddling vitamins and elixirs—but it took giving up on so-called miracle cures for me to stumble on a *real* one: the most powerful cure-all known to man."

"You don't know that," Fable said. "You can't know how it will affect people."

"I didn't know," Hill admitted. "Not at first. I didn't understand what I had found, but then I cut my hand on a broken jar, and the next thing I knew I was smashing my desk through the side of that inn like it was made of tissue paper. It only took the faintest tap."

"*You* smashed the inn?"

"I thought I must have imagined it. But I began to put the pieces together. The giant who destroyed my drill— the little devils who kept getting in my way when I went to rebuild it . . . Monsters don't protect treasure that isn't worth protecting. That powder had done something to me—it was powerful, and if this horrible forest was protecting it, then I needed to understand *why*. I needed more. I needed to conduct further tests."

"No," said Fable. "What you needed to do was give it back."

"You used Mr. Warner as a guinea pig!" said Cole. "That's why you kept hanging around them. You were testing your secret formula on Evie's dad!"

"It's not like that." Hill scowled and shook his head. "I didn't give him anything I hadn't already tested on myself. I like Oliver. I helped him. And what I learned from helping him will help so many more. Even with just a diluted suspension, Oliver has made an astounding recovery in record time. His leg was shattered. Shattered! Days later, and it's nearly healed! You can't begin to comprehend what that means! If only I could resume my work, obtain enough of the substance to produce—"

"But you couldn't," said Fable. "You couldn't get any more. Not with my forest getting in your way."

Hill's expression darkened. "No," he said. "That's true. I couldn't."

"You *wanted* this war," Fable said. "You wanted the town to be afraid of monsters so you could have an excuse to push them away from your drill site, didn't you? You let them *think* the forest started this, but it was you all along."

"Evie's journals," Cole breathed. "She told us you liked her pictures—Evie showed you her journals, didn't she? She showed you everything you needed to know to scare the town senseless and blame the forest. Sketches of gremlin tracks, Old Jim's tricks for catching pixies—all of it. You staged it, didn't you?"

Hill did not deny the accusation. He took a deep breath. *"Turn their strengths into your strength,* that's what my old man said." With a flick of his thumb, he popped the cork out of the slender vial.

"Don't—" Fable began, but her words were too late.

Hill tossed the contents of the vial down his throat and smashed the glass behind him on the stump. His whole body shuddered almost at once. His eyes closed tightly and he gritted his teeth. He was breathing heavily, and the vein on the side of his neck throbbed.

Fable stared as a vaporous double image hovered over the man, fading to wisps as it grew. Hill drew in a long, deep breath and opened his eyes. His pupils were enormous, nearly all the color of his eyes lost to their blackness. "That's better. Just the extra kick I might need to dispose of a pair of wild *creatures* before you ruin everything."

TWENTY-NINE

Tinn leaned heavily on a slim scrap of lumber Evie had pulled from the wreckage for him. Pain shot through his ankle as he moved, but he had to know what was happening. The clamor of battle had been frightening, but the sudden and absolute silence was worse.

"Careful," said Evie as he hobbled to the opening in the wild-wall.

"I'm okay—" he grunted, but the moment he tried to put weight on the leg, it betrayed him. He stumbled, and Evie caught his arm.

"What's going on out there?" he managed when he was steady again.

"I don't know," said Evie. "Everybody's gone except for Cole and Fable and Mr. Hill. They're just . . . talking."

Tinn peered out through the gap. "Something . . . doesn't feel right," he said.

"Has *any* of this felt right?" Evie said. She squeezed through to see what Tinn was seeing. "Does Mr. Hill look . . . bigger to you?" she whispered.

And then in a burst of motion, Jacob Hill reached down from the tree stump and hauled Fable up roughly by the neck.

Evie gasped.

"No!" Tinn yelled.

They watched as Cole leapt up after her—but Hill batted him away with an iron rod, and Cole spun heavily to the ground.

"We have to do something!" Evie scanned her feet and reached to pick up a sturdy piece of wood to use as a weapon. It wasn't even half the width of the beam that had crushed Tinn's leg, but her arms quavered as she tried to lift it. She could barely get it off the ground, and once she had, she dropped it with a heavy *thud*. "I . . . I think it's wearing off already," she said. "I'm just me again."

"I have an idea," Tinn grunted.

Hill's fingers felt like steel around Fable's throat. She swung and kicked, but he held fast. Out of the corner of her eye, she saw Cole hit the ground hard on his side. She tried in vain to force Hill's fingers apart with her mind. She squeezed her eyes shut and struggled to summon a breeze or a web of vines, but the forest did not respond. *Ugh!* Why did magic have to be so *difficult*? She swung wide with both hands and then slapped them together beneath Hill's arm. A spray of sparks bounced feebly off of the man's chest.

He shook his head, unimpressed. "Is that the best you've got?"

Fable couldn't breathe. She felt her vision starting to dim. She struggled and scratched, but Hill's grip was too strong. She twisted and squirmed, and in a muffled *whumpf*, Hill found himself holding not a girl but a bear, fangs bared and fur bristling. Fable's transformation caught him off guard, and she clawed at his arms. He recoiled, and Fable tumbled backward, rolling off the stump onto the roots of the old Grandmother Tree, gasping for air.

Hill hopped down from the stump, taking unhurried steps as he approached the gasping cub. He regarded the rod in his hands. "Iron," he said. "Versatile material. Always liked it." Fable flinched as he bent the rod into a smooth U with a squeal of protesting metal. "Also good against many of your lot, or so I hear."

He lunged, and without enough time to scramble out of the way, Fable could only brace herself for the blow. Hill drove both ends of the rod into the dirt, piercing the ground on either side of her. She felt the cold metal press her down into the soil, stapling her to the earth. Her lungs protested under the pressure, and her arms were too tight against her sides to pull them free.

Hill's mouth twitched in a smile as she struggled, turning into a girl and back again to a bear in vain. It was no use. Fable was caught tight.

Cole's whole right side pulsed in agony with each beat of his heart. With tremendous effort, he pushed himself upright, ribbons of tight pain running up and down his side, meeting at his rib cage. "Ow," he groaned.

From the hills in front of him, he could see his neighbors, just beginning to venture back down the hillside. He turned his eyes to the forest, where tentative hooves and pads were moving out of the shadows once more. The spell holding both sides back appeared to have broken.

"Now stay put," Mr. Hill was saying.

Cole blinked. "Fable?" he called, weakly.

Hill straightened up, and his gaze turned to Cole. "Don't think I'm done with you," he said.

"Jacob?" called a voice from behind them.

As one, Hill and Cole turned to watch Oliver Warner hobble forward, his cane catching here and there on the rocky terrain.

"Oliver? What in blazes are you doing here?" Hill's voice was tight, and Cole could sense his fear. Hill's whole plan hinged on the townspeople believing that he was the noble hero. But if Mr. Warner learned the truth—if he knew Hill had manufactured the whole thing . . .

"Mr. Warner," wheezed Cole. "You have to stop him!"

"Don't listen to him," said Hill. "Don't trust either of them, whatever they say."

"I . . . I don't understand," said Mr. Warner. "These are Evie's friends."

"They only want you to think that," insisted Hill, urgently. "They are beasts!"

"I . . . I thought I saw that one turn into an animal," Mr. Warner said.

"That's right, she did!" Hill nodded. "Believe the evidence of your own eyes, my friend, not what these monsters would have you believe. They are the worst sort of deceivers!"

"Don't listen to him!" Fable growled from the dirt. "He's lying! He caused all of this! He's a bad man!"

"See what I mean?" Hill shook his head. "Feeble, obvious lies, but sinister ones if you allow them to poison your mind. Now, really, Oliver, what are you doing here? You're in no shape for a fight."

"I just wanted to help." Mr. Warner took another wobbly step forward, glancing at Cole nervously.

"You were *already* helping me, Oliver," Hill said with the barely patient tone that a parent uses on a child. "I told you to keep an eye on those containers, remember? It's not safe for you to be out here, and it's not safe for those samples to be left unguarded."

The powder! Cole's heat beat faster, and his chest throbbed all the more painfully.

Mr. Warner nodded and allowed himself to be turned around. He leaned heavily on Hill's shoulder, his leg nearly giving out on him. "Yes. I remember now. I'm sorry."

"Wait," Cole wheezed.

"It's fine, Oliver. It's fine." Hill's lips were tight as he supported Mr. Warner by the arm, urging him away from the field and up toward the hills again. "Just get yourself back home now. Can you manage that?"

"Of course." Warner nodded. "Right away, sir. Just remind me where those samples are and I'll go see to them."

"Oh, for—" Hill pinched the bridge of his nose. "The

steamer trunk, Oliver. They are in my steamer trunk right at the foot of your—"

Hill stopped talking abruptly. He released Warner's shoulder and stepped back a pace, his eyes narrowing. Oliver Warner wobbled. He looked increasingly nervous under Hill's scrutinizing gaze.

"Wrong leg," Hill said.

"Oh, that. Yeah," said Mr. Warner. Except suddenly his voice did not sound like Evie's father's. He sounded much too young. Warner's features blurred and wobbled like the far end of a road on a hot summer day, and his face transformed into Tinn's face. "I was hoping maybe you wouldn't notice." Tinn shrugged feebly. "Not sure how much longer I could've kept it up, anyway."

The sunlight caught a hint of glass in the changeling's hand and Hill patted his jacket reflexively. "You little thief," he said, but he sounded almost impressed. "You've stolen one of my vials."

"Noticed that, too, huh?" Tinn swallowed. "Evie! Egg toss!"

He whipped the glass tube high over Hill's head. It sailed across the field until it came to land in the cupped hands of Evie Warner.

"Run!" Tinn shouted. Evie nodded and bolted away over the uneven terrain.

Hill snarled. "You," he spat, kicking the makeshift cane out from under Tinn and giving him a shove. The boy crumpled to the ground beside his brother. ". . . Are beginning to test my patience."

Hill sneered down at them, and then something in the grass caught his eye. He leaned down and picked up Old Jim's discarded rifle. The barrel opened with a click. "Just one shot," he said, snapping it closed again. "Choices, choices."

Annie Burton raced down the hill. The entire town had just watched Tinn transform. They had felt Fable's power. There would be no hiding them after this. So much for secrets.

"You see what we're up against?" Jacob Hill was yelling from the center of the field. In his hands he held a gleaming rifle. "They will stop at nothing to manipulate you!"

Annie's stomach lurched. Hill's contagious zeal had turned maniacal. His eyes looked eerily black. She ran faster.

"They are shape-shifters, my friends! Demons! They are—"

"My boys!" Annie cried. "Stop! Please!" She was still so far away, her legs pumping as she raced over the scarred landscape.

Hill glowered, but then his face became a mask of indulgent sympathy, and he addressed the hills all the more loudly. "This poor woman has suffered enough, ladies and gentlemen. She has been under the thrall of these monsters for too long. *All* of you have!" He lifted the rifle and drew back the hammer. "But that ends now."

"NO!" Annie yelled.

Fable screamed.

It was the scream that did it. The queen had already nearly reached the stump of the Grandmother Tree when she heard it. She pulled the cloak over her head as she ran. In a blur of motion, a mountain of furry muscles, sharp fangs, and wicked claws was suddenly barreling toward Jacob Hill. The queen roared.

Mr. Hill spun, the loaded rifle in his hands, the hammer drawn.

The bear leapt.

Hill pulled the trigger.

The gun went off with a ferocious *BANG*.

Fable did not stop screaming, not even after the air had left her lungs. It was a scream beyond sound.

274

She watched in horror as her mother's body jerked back midair as if caught on an invisible wire. She watched the unstoppable Queen of the Deep Dark drop like a bear-shaped boulder into the dirt at Hill's feet.

Then there was stillness—there was the echo of that lone gunshot bouncing across the hills—and there was the screaming. The screaming was everywhere. It made Fable's vision reel. It came from every tree, every rock, every blade of grass. The forest was screaming with her.

And Fable could hear it. She could hear the forest, clear as day.

She couldn't *not* hear it—it was deafening.

And the forest heard Fable, as well.

And their cries were one cry.

And then the earth moved.

THIRTY

REALITY BENT.

The hillside rolled like waves in a storm, throwing wary combatants off of their feet before they had even rejoined the fight. The entire horizon had become a writhing serpent. Raw power crackled in the air like lightning.

Fable did not remember rising, but she was suddenly upright and free, the soil no longer pressing into her back. Many days later, a confused hinkypunk would find a warped iron rod lodged deeply in the trunk of a mossy tree three miles away. The hinkypunk—not knowing that the twisted metal had once restrained the most powerful being in the Wild Wood—would use it to hang wild garlic for drying.

Fable filled her lungs. High above her, dark clouds began to churn. She slid her foot forward and the ground beneath her swelled in response. She clenched her fists, and a hundred knotty roots writhed like serpents under her feet. She and the forest spoke wordlessly, connected by an understanding beyond language.

Jacob Hill dropped the smoking rifle.

Fable's eyes narrowed, and vines erupted from the earth like geysers, whipping around Hill's wrists. With a yowl, he ripped his arms free just as a fresh tangle of roots wrapped themselves around his legs. He kicked wildly, tearing loose again, the strength of a giant still coursing through his veins.

Hill glowered at the girl, his gaze like fire. He took a step toward her, uprooting creeping plants each time he moved. Another step. A third. The wind whipped across the field and Fable's vegetative assault increased. Hill's progress slowed. He was strong, but Fable and the forest were relentless. For a moment they seemed to have reached a stalemate.

Then Hill ripped a hand free and plunged it into his jacket pocket. He drew out not just one but a whole handful of delicate glass vials. He must have had at least half a dozen left, the glimmering powder shining like diamonds inside the tubes. A scratchy howl rang out in the field below—first one spriggan, then two, and soon dozens were crying out in rage and indignation at the sight of the remains clutched in Hill's unworthy hands.

Hill ignored the noise. He reached to uncork a vial, but Fable caught his free hand with a whippy vine and held it back. "I think you've had enough," she said.

Hill tugged against the winding cord, but his power was waning. With his free hand, he drew the vials to his mouth and ripped the wax off one of them with his teeth—but before he could tip the precious powder into his mouth, another leafy vine yanked that arm back. He shuddered with effort as he tried to pull free, but the cords held tight to both wrists now.

Hill was trapped, his chest heaving, his feet barely visible within a tangled web of roots that climbed nearly to his knees, his arms pulled tight in opposite directions. Struggle all he might, the restraints held fast.

Fable panted. Her arms fell limp at her sides. The earth settled once more, and the winds died away. With weary, stumbling steps, she staggered at last to the figure lying still and silent on the broken earth.

Head swimming, Fable collapsed to her knees at her

mother's side. She could still feel the heat rising from the woman's body.

Get up, she thought. *Move.*

Hot, heavy tears ran down her cheeks, but Fable could not seem to find the strength to wipe them away. *Get up. Please.*

Her chest began to shake with heavy sobs. Fable could hear her mother's voice, chiding her. *You are the future queen of this forest, and it is long past time you began to act like it.* The memory only made it worse.

In spite of his unyielding position, Hill's lips drew back in a sneer and he laughed. The sound made Fable's stomach turn. She heard a soft *crunch* and a tinkle of glass.

"This isn't over yet," the man whispered.

Numbly, Fable turned. She blinked away hot tears.

Blood was dripping from Hill's closed fist. He grimaced and clenched his fingers around the wet shards.

Fable's mind struggled to make sense of what she was seeing. Her eyes widened. The vials. He'd crushed them all at once. Their contents were now coursing straight through Hill's bloodstream. Jacob Hill began to shudder.

Evie scrambled over the broken earth as quickly as she could. The skies boiled above her. She could hear Mr.

Hill's furious growls behind her, but she dared not look back. The man she thought she knew was gone, replaced by something awful. Her searching eyes finally locked on to a miniature gray figure in the dust ahead.

Flinty tore his eyes away from the battle as Evie neared.

"You," the spriggan rasped.

"Me," panted Evie, and with one hand she reverently held out the vial.

Flinty's eyes widened. He looked at the tube, his deep scowl carving hard lines into the rocky ridges of his brow. "You know what it is?" he asked, his voice barely a whisper.

"I know," said Evie. "And I know what it does."

The spriggan drew in a sharp breath, his beady eyes narrowing in indignation.

"It was an accident," Evie explained. "But I felt it. It made me strong."

Flinty's scowl deepened.

"I didn't know what it was," said Evie. "But I understand now. I'm sorry."

The field had fallen silent once more as Flinty reached gingerly up and took the vial from Evie. The tube was easily half his height, but he held it like it might blow away in the wind at any moment.

"We'll help you get the rest back, too," said Evie. "I promise."

He eyed her suspiciously. "You will help us defeat the humans?"

"No," Evie said. "Not like that. Not through fighting."

The spriggan's lips sank into a scowl.

"Listen," Evie insisted. "Those people didn't know. None of this is their fault. Well, except for one of them. You don't need to defeat *all* the humans. Just help me stop that one."

Behind her, in the distance, there came the quiet tinkling of glass and a cruel laugh. Evie looked over her shoulder just in time to see the transformation.

Jacob Hill shook. He bellowed—it was a raw, animal sound of pain and wrath and unbridled power. It echoed across the hills. A ghostly apparition materialized around his body, and then it was no mere glimmer of light, but a material form, growing and bulging outward, solidifying until it was as dense as rock and as tall as a pine tree. The vines that had held him prisoner now snapped and fell away like cheap twine. The enormous figure that towered over the clearing looked like Hill, but also like something else at the same time—a grotesque, inhuman version of the man he had been.

"Just one?" rasped Flinty.

"Yep." Evie gulped. "Guess which one."

Fable stood up. Hill was four stories tall, his body hideous and undulating, too much magic trying to contain itself in too small a package. A fist like a slab of granite slammed into Fable before she saw it coming, and suddenly the girl was airborne. She was falling, tumbling through empty air, plummeting toward the Wild Wood. As she fell, her mind cleared.

The forest caught Fable. The ground rose to meet her, and she landed gently on her feet. She swayed for only a moment and wiped her nose. It was bleeding, but only a little. She was going to have a wicked bruise later. It was oddly peaceful here, just a short way from the battlefield. The monstrous figure of Jacob Hill was visible over the treetops, silhouetted against the white smoke of the battlefield.

"Thanks, trees," Fable breathed.

The branches rustled.

"You ready?" she said.

A pinecone bounced off her shoulder and landed beside her.

"Me, too." Fable cracked her knuckles. "Let's do this."

"Too much," Flinty croaked. His eyes were frozen on the giant Jacob Hill.

"Then make yourself big again!" Evie urged. "Stop him! You're supposed to protect the forest, right?"

Flinty took a deep breath and made a hollow clicking sound with the back of his throat. Within seconds, a pair of spriggan sentries had materialized on his left and right. He gave them each a short chirp and a solemn nod. They bowed and then reverently removed the tiniest pinch of powder from each of their war satchels. As one, they threw back their heads and swallowed the glittering shards before vanishing again into the tall grasses.

Evie looked back at Flinty. "What about you? Aren't you going to make yourself giant, too?"

"Cannot." Flinty's face was even harder than usual. Evie couldn't tell if the expression was misery or fury. "Mine is already spent."

"What do you mean? You've got a whole big vial of it right in your hands!"

"Cannot. *Must* not." Flinty shook his head wretchedly. "Too much makes us wrong—makes us forget who we are."

Evie swallowed. "You think Mr. Hill remembers who he is right now?"

Flinty turned a solemn gaze back to the grotesque Jacob Hill and shook his head.

Tinn tried to stand and crumpled at once. Jolts of pain hammered into his leg like nails. He closed his eyes and took a deep breath. The earth rumbled with every movement of the monstrous Jacob Hill.

"You okay?" groaned a voice beside him.

Tinn opened his eyes. Cole was holding his own chest as he crept closer. His brother's face looked pale and his movements were stiff.

"I'm good," Tinn lied. "Just need . . . a minute. You?"

"I'm great," Cole wheezed. He came to a rest at Tinn's elbow, breathing in short, shallow gulps.

Tinn let the back of his head sink down against the cold, rocky ground. Fable was gone. The queen was gone. It was just the two of them left on the battlefield. And the monster Hill.

A bellowing roar echoed across the clearing, triumphant, cruel, and cackling. The creature that had once been Jacob Hill returned his attention to the twins. In a single step, he was looming over them, burying the boys in his shadow. He raised a knee to crush them, like insects, beneath one enormous foot.

Tinn held his breath. Cole held his brother's hand.

Tinn glanced at him, and the two of them tightened their grip. There would be no running. No fighting. There would just be the two of them until the end.

A deafening crash followed . . . but not the crash the twins expected.

The hulking Hill was stumbling backward, and he was suddenly not the only giant on the field. A second massive figure had appeared. This one was earthen and covered in moss, muscular, but not quite as large as Jacob Hill. The spriggan colossus cried out in fury and drove a hard blow into Hill's chest before the man could properly regain his balance.

Hill swung a wild punch as he stumbled, smacking the mossy giant back a pace just as a second spriggan sprang up beside it, covered in a hide of thick brown bark like wooden armor. One of the wooden giant's legs moved stiffly, and Tinn squinted up at it to see that its enormous calf appeared to have been set into a splint the same color as the creature's skin.

"That one's injured," Tinn whispered.

Cole breathed in through gritted teeth. "Yeah," he whispered back. "I think maybe I had something to do with that."

The two massive spriggans charged toward Hill together, the ground shaking with the force of the ensuing blows. From either side of the clearing, eyes widened as humans and forest folk alike watched the giants slug it out. It was two against one, but Hill was easily ten feet taller than either spriggan, his chest bulging and his arms as thick as tree trunks. Again and again, he brushed off their most brutal attacks. Again and again he drove the towering brawlers to their knees. As powerful as they were, it quickly became clear that even they could not subdue Jacob Hill.

The forest parted ahead of Fable. The soil beneath her feet swelled with each step to support her, propel her, and launch her with royal rage back into the fray.

A crowd of shellycoats and dryads lingering near the forest's edge gave out startled gasps as the girl rocketed past them and emerged once again on the desolate battle-ground. A rippling wave of lush moss and green grass spread out in her wake, ferns and flowers sprouting from each footstep—but Fable did not notice the fresh growth. Her eyes were on the monster that loomed ahead.

Jacob Hill—or what was left of Jacob Hill—laughed as a mossy spriggan crumpled under his attacks. The power flowing through him was everything. They had tried to keep this from him—and now they were trying to take it back. But the power was his now, and he would make them pay for interfering. The whole world would bow before him.

"Hey, stupid!"

Hill looked down. The girl did not come up to his knees. His grotesque lips curled back in a smile.

And then Fable clapped, just once.

The result was not a spark so much as a blast of lightning. The crackling explosion sent Hill spinning backward. He landed hard on his chest, draped over the Grandmother Stump. The smell of burnt hair hung in the air.

"Hold him." Fable's voice was calm and even.

The spriggans were on Hill in an instant, pinning him down. He struggled, growling like a trapped beast.

The stump beneath him shuddered. All around him, the wood began to grow.

Hill threw an elbow at the mossy giant, who endured the blow and kept a solid hold. They secured Hill in place as Fable and the Wild Wood poured all of their energy into that tree.

The old oak grew. Its trunk rose, pressing into Hill's chest, tentatively at first, and then wrapping around him like a river pouring up into the sky. Branches sprouted, and the wood creaked and groaned as it expanded.

Hill shouted and shook, but his limbs had less and less room to move as the tree grew dense and wide around him, encasing him in a natural prison. The spriggans did not waver. They held firm, even as the wood encased them, too. First their arms and then their bodies were enveloped by the oak. Gradually, they began to fade, their outlines flickering into mist, but by then the tree had imprisoned Hill beyond escape. A miniscule mossy figure flittered down one side of the new oak tree, and one with skin like bark flittered down the other side.

The tree was even thicker now than it had been before it was cut down. Leaves sprouted above them in a dense green canopy, and the whole clearing was suddenly washed in cool greens. Hill's face, a mask of rage, hung in the center of the trunk like a grotesque, lumpy knot.

"You—" he grunted, but the bark closed in over his mouth before he could finish the thought. His nostrils flared as he glared at Fable.

The field fell quiet at last.

"That should hold you," Fable said softly. "Until the powder has time to wear off."

"He won't be the same," a raspy voice from behind her declared. Fable turned to see Evie stepping over a fresh bed of lush green moss. On her shoulder sat a flinty spriggan.

"Not ever," Flinty continued. "It makes you wrong. Makes you not yourself. He took too much. Went too far."

Fable nodded. Everything had gone too far. And nothing would ever be the same again. Her feet began moving before she knew where they were taking her. Numbly, she crossed in front of the new Grandmother Tree. Her mother's body was still there at its roots, somehow untouched by the chaos of the fight.

Her mother looked as if she could be resting. Fable could almost believe she was still breathing. A knot rose in her throat and the world suddenly blurred with hot tears.

"Are . . . are we still fighting?" a voice called from somewhere in the hills to her left.

"No more fighting!" Fable cried. "Everybody *lost*. You all lost because you're all angry and stupid and . . . and . . ." She swallowed.

All eyes turned to the girl. Her mouth felt dry. Her mother would know what to say in a moment like this. The Queen of the Deep Dark would have stood with her chin up and her cloak waving in the breeze, and she would have spoken firmly and eloquently, and then everything would have been okay. Fable didn't know how to make everything okay—she only knew how to get everything wrong.

Suddenly her mother's words hung in the back of her mind. She sniffed, and lifted her chin. "And in the end, maybe we can all learn more from how we got it wrong than we might have learned from getting it right."

The collected masses were all staring at Fable. She had never felt smaller.

"It's okay to have your own special places and to be your own special selves," she pressed on. "Everybody needs that. But you can have that and still be a part of something bigger."

General Pholon took several steps out of the forest. At his hooves, the gnomes crept forward as well.

"Look, spriggans and trolls and centaurs—you have never exactly gotten along, but you're here now, aren't you? You all belong to your own groups, but you are also a part of the Wild Wood, and the Wild Wood is a part of you. It's *not* just a bunch of stupid trees. It's a place to belong." The leaves rustled in the wind. "*That* is what's worth protecting."

"We will defend it fiercely," Flinty grunted, "as we always have." He slipped down from Evie's arm and landed on the ground at Fable's feet. "It is the humans who do not belong."

"You're wrong." Fable drew a deep breath. "Endsborough—and all the humans in Endsborough—are a part of the Wild Wood, too."

Murmurs erupted in the crowds to either side.

"They've always been a part of us," Fable continued. "A long time ago, someone drew a bunch of imaginary lines, and somehow we all forgot they were imaginary. We forgot that those people are a part of our world and they forgot that we're a part of theirs."

Flinty's beady eyes narrowed. "The queen has always respected those lines," he hissed. Fable's chest tightened. "The Old Queen even helped draw some of them."

"Maybe," said Fable. "But she crossed them, too. Right here. That's what this place is." The light filtering through the leaves of the new Grandmother Tree caressed Fable's face. "This was not a place to look out for enemies—it was a place to look out for one another. It was a place where my grandmother could belong to both worlds. And maybe it can be like that again."

Fable's eyes swept from the fair folk and the wildlings to the humans, timidly emerging from the rolling hills. "You *do* belong here. All of you. And because you belong here, you're going to need to learn *how* to belong together. You're going to have to learn how to respect each other—even if you never understand each other. You're all going to need to respect each other's imaginary lines, and be patient as they learn how to respect yours."

"What does that mean?" someone yelled.

"It means we might not always like each other, but humans had better be a lot nicer when they see a pixie stuck in a shop window, and forest folk better be a lot nicer when they see a human lost in the woods. It means that, from now on, we remember that if something threatens Endsborough, it threatens the Wild Wood, and if something threatens the Wild Wood, it threatens Endsborough. We look out for each other. I can't promise monsters like Mr. Hill won't try to hurt the forest again or that forest creatures won't threaten the town, but from here on out we deal with them *together*."

"Hm," Flinty grunted, unsatisfied. "And what will become of the villain Hill?" He nodded up at the parts of the grotesque giant that still stuck out of the wide oak. "Once the magic has worn off, who will have the honor of delivering his death?"

"Nobody," said Fable.

Flinty narrowed his eyes again. "Do you lack the strength to finish this?"

"Violence and strength aren't the same thing," said Fable. "Besides, you told me yourself—that powder makes you wrong. It makes you not yourself. Well, you didn't tell Mr. Hill that, did you? He didn't know what he had found or what it was doing to him. Maybe if we had just talked to each other and helped each other understand instead of keeping secrets and smashing things, then none of this would have happened. Everything Mr. Hill did today was wrong, yes, but his death won't make it right."

"The man will *never* be right," said Flinty.

"Maybe not. But I still forbid any of you from killing him. There's been enough violence." Her eyes flicked to the place where her mother's body lay, and her throat tightened.

"She *forbids* it?" Flinty said. His brow rose.

There was tense silence across the field, and then, slowly, the flinty spriggan took to one knee.

"The queen forbids it," he said.

The queen. The title ran through Fable like a stab of electricity. It felt prickly and wrong and it made her shoulders tighten. All the confidence she had mustered for the speech suddenly wanted to leak out through the corners of her eyes. Fable did not want to be queen. She wanted her mother.

THIRTY-ONE

A BULLET IS SUCH A SMALL THING WITH SUCH A short life—but all lives are short in the end. So little time to get it right.

From the moment the bullet left the barrel of Old Jim's rifle, it had done everything right. It had been aimed directly for the woman's heart. She had been a bear when it found her. That might have surprised the bullet, if a bullet knew the difference between a bear and a woman—but it was the same heart in the end. It was the same life.

The bullet had flown straight and true, the wind parting on either side of it—and for just a fraction of a second, it had come alive. In that fleeting fragment of a moment, the bullet had awoken, and it had felt something.

And *what* the bullet had felt . . . was a nudge.

Chief Nudd's magic could not bend the forest to his will. He was no Witch of the Wood, after all—he was only a humble goblin. But a goblin could give a small thing a small nudge.

At exactly the right time.

Raina opened her eyes.

The world was a blur of harsh light and confusing shadows. The first thing she felt was pain—a sharp throbbing ache in her chest. Close on the heels of pain came confusion.

Where was she? Where was Fable?

She could feel soft sheets around her and a pillow under her head. The air smelled like wool and cat hair and freshly baked bread. She took shallow breaths, her chest impossibly tight. Slowly, Raina's vision slid into focus. Sunlight filtered into the room through pale curtains. A room. She was in a room, on a bed. Her bearskin cloak hung over the back of a chair beside her.

She sat up—*tried* to sit up—and was immediately overwhelmed by a piercing pang like a lance being driven through her chest. She fell back on the soft mattress again until the room stopped spinning and she could think.

Where was Fable?

The door creaked and Raina turned her head weakly toward the sound. Annie Burton crossed the soft carpet to her bedside.

"Good morning," she said, relief in her eyes. "You're going to be okay—but I wouldn't try to get up just yet."

Raina drew breath to respond, but the soreness pulsed through her lungs and she said nothing instead.

"Dr. Fisher says the bullet missed your heart by about an inch. It grazed a rib and planted itself snug against your lung. You're lucky to be alive."

"Unh," Raina managed.

"Well, as lucky as a person can be when they've just been shot in the chest, I suppose. Probably helped that you were a bear when it happened. The bullet might have done more damage if you had been human at the time."

Questions swam around Raina's mind. *How long have I been sleeping? How did I get here? Where is here? Where is Fable?* She managed a wheezy "H-how . . . long?"

"You've been sleeping for two days. I'll be putting some soup in you as soon as you feel up to eating."

Two days? Raina reeled. Two days! She couldn't afford

to leave the forest for two *minutes*, not with everything spiraling out of control. The pixies and the spriggans and—

"Stay still." Annie put a gentle hand on her shoulder. "You're not going anywhere right now. You need time to heal."

"F-Fable," Raina managed. "Where is . . . Fable?"

"Fable is fine. More than fine, actually; she's doing remarkably well. You should be proud of your daughter. She turned that field in the hills into a sort of neutral meeting place—not exactly part of the woods, but not properly part of the town, either. She's spent most of the past two days supervising things—whenever she isn't right here watching over you, that is. She checks in every few hours to see if you're up yet."

"She's there now? Alone?"

"Never alone. The boys have been with her nonstop, and Chief Nudd lent a few goblin guards to help her keep the peace, just in case anybody decides to get ornery—but as far as I've seen, they've all been on their best behavior. She made it pretty clear that she wasn't going to tolerate any sort of mischief. You should've heard her threaten the gnomes. She reminds me of you, actually. Heck, she's even kept my boys out of trouble for two days straight, so I suspect there must be some sort of magic involved."

"Fable . . . is giving orders?" Raina said.

"Lots of them," Annie chuckled. "Smart ones, too. She's good at it. And having a chance to meet the so-called enemy face-to-face has taken the edge off of a lot of people's fear and panic. Evie Warner has been particularly popular up there, the darling. She showed some pixies a few of the pictures she had drawn, and they insisted on posing for better ones. All manner of creatures have been taking turns sitting for portraits all day. The girl's quite an artist. A troll called Kurrg seemed particularly pleased with how his came out. Evie let him keep it."

"Kurrg?" Raina breathed. "Kurrg the Ruthless?"

"It all sounds mad, I know, but two days ago Endsborough and the Wild Wood were at each other's throats, and yesterday I watched Albert Townshend teach some sort of hobgoblin how to play marbles. Jim Warner apologized to a pixie. I don't think I've ever seen that man apologize to a human. Your daughter did that. I'm still not sure how she managed it—but she did."

"They're . . . listening?" Raina said. "To Fable?"

"More than listening. They're calling her Little Queen."

Raina laid her head back on the pillow. The trees rustled contentedly in the breeze outside. She smiled. It had been a long time since Raina had slept on a proper mattress in a proper house. *Little Queen*. Perhaps the forest really could manage without her—at least for a while.

THIRTY-TWO

A COOL BREEZE CARRIED THE GENTLE BREATH of pines and wild lavenders across the field. The remains of Mr. Hill's equipment had been reduced to dark lumps that hugged the earth, already overtaken by ivy and moss, thanks to Fable's strong encouragement.

Leaves rustled high in the branches of the Grandmother Tree. Fable's tree. Mr. Hill was no longer trapped within it. It had taken hours, but the powder had finally worn off and he had shrunk back to his regular size. He had been moved—pale, shivering, and mumbling incoherently—to a cell in the town's jailhouse. The spriggans had not been happy about that. A crime had been committed against them, after all, and they felt they should have some say in the consequences—but they had not pressed the matter.

Great big knots scarred the tree where the giant had been. They would heal eventually, but in the meantime, children from the village had already discovered that a good round rock tossed in at the top would come rattling out through one of the leg holes, and they had wasted no time designing games based on guessing where objects might emerge. While digging around in the grass for good tossing stones, Peggy Washington found a smooth, polished moss agate. The unexpected treasure brought a smile to her face.

The shadow of Fable's tree stretched over the field like a yawning cat in the afternoon light. There should have been bodies. Everyone agreed that there should have been countless casualties after all that fighting—and yet, impossibly, there were none. Dr. Fisher had busied herself to exhaustion over the past few days trying to keep it that way, treating burns and stitching cuts. Some of the elders found this happy fact unsettling. That much blood does not spill without catching Death's attention. But so it was. The grass would grow wildly well the following season.

And so the only bodies occupying the field as Raina stepped gingerly into it for the first time since the battle were healthy and whole, sitting around a handful of dwindling campfires and sipping cider, telling stories, and laughing.

Fable held Raina's arm to steady her. "I've got you, Mama."

Raina breathed in the blending aroma of subtle perfumes, pipe tobacco, and pine needles, all dancing together in the air. "Okay, *Little Queen*," she said. "Show me."

"Oh! Do another!" Hana Sakai clapped her hands.

Tinn took a deep breath and concentrated. His chin wavered for a moment, and then out sprouted a big, bushy beard that consumed the bottom half of his face.

"That one's Mr. Zervos!" Eunice called out.

"Too easy," said Oscar. "Do another!"

"Do Mrs. Silva!"

"No, do Old Jim!"

It felt strange. Not the peculiar tingling that came with each transformation—Tinn was finally getting used to that—no, it felt strange to have the weight of his big secret suddenly gone. It felt impossible to be standing in a field in the center of all his classmates, not hiding anything.

Tinn had braced himself for fear and hate for so

long—he had never taken the time to even consider the possibility of acceptance.

"Oh! That's Sheriff Stroud!" Oscar yelled.

Even bratty Rosalie Richmond had joined the circle. "*That* was supposed to be Sheriff Stroud?" She rolled her eyes. "That was your worst one yet. It didn't look *anything* like him."

In that moment, Tinn could have hugged her. It was all so inexplicably, beautifully *normal*. Tinn was *himself.* No secrets. Everything out in the open.

He closed his eyes and took another deep breath. "Okay. How about this?"

Kull watched from the edge of the field. He could not stop smiling. Tinn was the rarest goblin in a generation—maybe the rarest in history—and he was finally giving himself up to it completely. He was showing the humans, and they were clapping and patting him on the back! It was more than Kull had ever dared hope for the wee changeling he had carried across the mire all those years ago. His heart swelled with pride.

"Go on, then," said Chief Nudd beside him. "Say hello, at least."

Kull turned toward the chief, horrified.

"Yer allowed," Nudd assured him. "This place is common ground."

Kull bit his lip. "I wouldn'a want ta ruin it," he said. "I'd only embarrass him. He's a right wonder, he is, puttin' on all them faces—but I've only got the one face, an' I'm fair sure it's na one the lad wants his wee friends ta see."

"Kull!"

Kull froze. Tinn had spotted him.

"I think yer lad might have his own ideas about who he wants his wee friends ta see," said Nudd with a wink.

Kull's legs instinctively prepared to run away, but a gentle push from behind sent him stumbling forward, instead.

"These are my friends," said Tinn. "Everybody, this is Kull. Goblin parents are . . . more complicated than human parents, but he's basically my goblin dad."

Kull's vision went blurry. He wiped his eyes with the back of his arm.

"Do you think it would be okay," Tinn asked, "for us to show my friends a howl?"

Fable held her mother's hand as they crossed the field. Raina allowed herself a smile as Kull and Tinn started in on a raucous old shanty about highway robbers and floating islands. It was all in Goblish, but the children huddled around them didn't seem to mind.

Evie Warner was regaling a hob with the story of her very own honest-to-goodness adventure in the Wild Wood. She sketched the fellow as she talked, and every now and then he leaned in to see her progress. Raina glanced over the child's shoulder. The face grinning up from Evie's sketchbook was plump and wrinkled with a long, crooked nose. Beneath wiry brows, his eyes were kind and bright. It was a good likeness.

"Are you okay, Mama?" Fable said.

Raina wiped a tear from the corner of her eye. "I was so worried I wouldn't get to see the sort of queen you would become." She put a hand on her daughter's cheek. "You are a good Witch of the Wood, Fable."

Fable leaned in to her mother's touch. "Only for the time being," she said. "You'll be better soon, and then all these butts can be your problem again. Come on. We're almost there. I want you to meet somebody."

An old woman with wispy white hair sat waiting in the smooth roots of the Grandmother Tree. Her eyes twinkled as she watched a group of children race around the trunk with a pair of giggling wood nymphs.

She looked up as Fable and her mother approached.

"Hello, my little hazelnut," the woman said. "Who's this?"

"Hi, Maggie," said Fable. "This is my mama. Mama, this is Maggie."

Old Mrs. Stewart put a hand to her chest. "Oh, my word," she whispered. "You do look just like her. You both do. I see it now." A curious smile grew at the corners of her mouth. "It's the eyes."

Raina looked at Fable for an explanation.

"You should ask her," Fable prompted, "about her lady."

"Now, *this* is how it ought to be," said Fable as Chief Nudd hopped up onto the mossy rock beside her. The two of them looked out across the field together. The sun was beginning to sink toward the horizon like a heavy head toward a pillow.

"Hm. Is it, though?" Nudd pursed his cracked lips.

Fable gave the chief a sideways glance. "Of course it is. Why? What do you mean?"

"Oh, it's nice," he added. "Right nice."

"It *is* nice." Fable scowled. "You don't think it *ought* to be nice?"

"Been in the world a long time, lass. I've known it ta be mad. Wicked. Beautiful. Never known it ta be nice." He

305

leaned back. "But if there was ever anyone in this not-so-nice world who could turn it inta exactly what she wanted it ta be—well, that'd be you."

Fable stared across the field. Evie had finished her drawing, and the hob applauded. Fable's mother and the old woman were still talking. "You can't just change the way things are," said Fable. "That's not how magic works."

"It's na the way yer *mother's* magic works," Nudd said. "I met a rather cross tortoise earlier who might argue that yer brand o' magic is a wee bit different."

Fable swallowed.

"Things change," Nudd said. "Big things. Little things. The whole world changes. All change is a sort o' magic. It isn'a always grand, and it isn'a always quick. But that doesn'a mean it isn'a magic."

Across the grass, Kull had begun coaching Cole through a valiant attempt at a goblin howl. It was terrible. Tinn was beside them, beaming.

"You, my wee witchy, are changin' the people around ya in ways ya dinna understand," Nudd continued. "An' yer lettin' them change you, too. Shifting of the tides." Nudd looked at Fable. The chief had a faint scar across one eye, and his skin looked like badly tanned leather, but somehow his expression was still soft. "Yer na yer mother, Fable. I'm na my father. We're the tides that *they* shifted. Now it's yer turn."

A game of checkers concluded and the gnomes cackled over their victory. Across the way, Hana's mother called her to go home. She waved goodbye to Kull and the twins, and was shortly followed by Oscar and Rosalie and all the rest. One by one the forest folk slipped back into the trees, and the humans headed back down the road toward their houses. Fable's mother and Mrs. Stewart looked like they were just about finished, too.

"I best collect Kull," Nudd said. "He looks a bit light-headed after all that excitement. Give yer mother my best, lass. We're all glad to see her on the mend." He slid down from the rock, and then added: "Sorry. Not *lass*. I mean . . . *Yer Majesty*." He gave Fable a cordial bow before padding away.

Fable breathed softly. The sky had warmed to a gentle orange-pink. She would only have to be queen for a little longer, and then her mother would be better. Until then, Fable was beginning to think that one day she really could do this queen thing—her own way. Maybe she really could make her world be what she wanted it to be.

Fable closed her eyes. She listened to the wind rustling through the branches, the chirp of crickets, and the hoot of an owl emerging for the evening. Fable listened to the forest—to *her* forest.

She listened. She breathed. She concentrated.

And she smiled.

EPILOGUE

CRICKETS CHIRPED IN THE TALL GRASS AS THE Burtons and the Witches of the Wood walked back toward town. Fable was asking Annie what sort of dress she was going to sew for her next, and Tinn was changing his skin color to match her descriptions. "Yeah, like that," said Fable. "But more dots. And the buttons in the front this time!"

Cole slowed, letting them walk a few paces ahead. The queen glanced down at him. The boy's brow was furrowed. "Something troubling you, child?" she asked.

Cole took a deep breath. "There's a pond," he said. "In the northern part of the Wild Wood. There's a girl there who can turn into a frog."

309

"Ah," said the woman. She took a deep breath. "What did Kallra show you?"

Reverently, Cole drew the slim stone from his pocket. He stared into it as if it might whisper secrets to him at any moment. The woman watched his thumb trace the etched lines on the artifact.

"Fable says Kallra's visions show the future," said Cole. "Is it true?"

"It is not healthy to dwell on the past, young man, nor to obsess about the future."

"But is it true?" Cole's voice cracked. "Because if it is, my father is still alive out there."

"I see." Raina pursed her lips.

Cole gave the stone a squeeze and then handed it to her. "What can you tell me about this?" he said.

She took the talisman and turned it over in the dim light.

"Is it a place?" Cole asked. "Or the sign of some secret group?"

"I'm sorry, Cole. I deal with nearly every faction in the Wild Wood, but I'm afraid I don't recognize this symbol."

"Neither did Fable," said Cole, sagging. Then, abruptly, he straightened. "But the spriggan did! The one I hit. He looked furious about it when he saw it. It meant something to him."

"You *struck* a spriggan?" Raina said. "You struck an *angry* spriggan?"

"The spriggans *have* to know what it means."

Raina regarded Cole's expression with concern. "Listen to me, child. You *cannot* seek out the spriggans," she said. "We have reached a truce in the wake of this latest catastrophe—but if you were to enter their domain, there is nothing either Fable or I could do to protect you. They may have called off the war, but their feelings about humans in the Wild Wood have not changed. You must know that it would be beyond reckless for you to intentionally enter their territory. They *will* kill you."

"I need to know."

Tenderly, Raina handed him back the stone. "I don't think there is anything *to* know," she said, softly. "I'm so sorry, Cole. If your father had been living somewhere in my forest for all these years, I would know about it."

Cole said nothing.

"Please," she added, "don't do anything foolish."

Cole nodded, but his jaw was set and his eyes were rimmed with red. He sniffed. Without responding, he stuffed the stone back in his pocket.

311

The forest trembled. Deep beneath the leaves and fallen pine needles of the Wild Wood—far below the reach of the winding roots and the sounds of chirping crickets, past the broken bones of slumbering giants, and deeper even than the ancient spriggan tunnels—Joseph Burton crept through heavy darkness.

ACKNOWLEDGMENTS

I must acknowledge Kat, you beautiful weirdo, without whom I could not write any of these books. Thank you for ALL of the things, forever.

I would also like to express my appreciation and admiration for my Wicked, Evil Stepmother. For several years, life has not so much given you lemons as it has fired lemons at you from a modified T-shirt cannon. That you continue to lob them back with force, cackling all the while, is both terrifying and inspiring. Keep cackling.